THE
THIEF
OF
BROKEN
TOYS

TIM LEBBON

ChiZine Publications

FIRST EDITION

The Thief of Broken Toys © 2010 by Tim Lebbon
Jacket design and photography © 2010 by Erik Mohr
All Rights Reserved.

LIBRARY AND ARCHIVES CANADA CATALOGUING IN PUBLICATION

Lebbon, Tim
The thief of broken toys / Tim Lebbon.

ISBN 978-0-9812978-9-7

I. Title.

PR6112.E26T55 2010   823.92   C2010-900686-0

CHIZINE PUBLICATIONS
Toronto, Canada
www.chizinepub.com
info@chizinepub.com

Edited by Brett Alexander Savory
Copyedited and proofread by Sandra Kasturi and Helen Marshall

Memory feeds imagination.
—Amy Tan

THE
THIEF
OF
BROKEN
TOYS

1

A bright, cold autumn day, and the village is living. People ebb and flow through its streets like a pulse, moving from here to there with familiar regularity. Some are tourists, but they're fewer in number now that the ice cream shops are closed and most of the self-catering cottages are wrapped up warm for the winter. Today has the feel of every familiar day. Down by the harbour we see a man stacking crates of just-landed fish onto a pallet, ready for the driver of a small forklift to transport into the big freezer behind the market. Soon, restaurant owners and shopkeepers will start milling and the fish will be brought out, displayed in their coffins of broken ice for inspection and purchase. Moving closer, drifting down on the low autumn sunbeams, we see the man more clearly.

He's tall, middle-aged, fit and strong, and

wearing skin leathered by years of exposure to the elements. There's a small scar across his left cheek, which he remembers putting there when he was barely into his teens—a clumsily cast fishing line, the hook spinning as it flicked by his face. He recalls the cool feeling of open skin, the surprise as he saw sunlight splashed red before his face, and then the tears of pain. It hurt at the time, but the scar has stood him in good stead over the years. It gives him character—even though he has more than enough character for one man—and more than one woman has ended up in his bed because of an interest in that scar. It draws the eye, dashed at a rakish angle across his cheek. And above it, his piercing blue eyes. His name is Jason, and he used to be your friend until he started sleeping with your wife.

You've never seen them together, not yet. Their affair is a whisper in the village, oft-repeated like the hush of the incoming tide on the small pebble beach. Jason feels sorry for you, and as he stacks three more crates, you cross his mind. He stands up and kneads the small of his back. It's been a long seven hours out at sea, and he's glad to be in for the day. He'll be going out again that evening, but in between will be sleep, a pint or two at the Old Anchor, and perhaps an hour with Elizabeth that afternoon. She loves him in the shower, swilling the salty tang from his skin while she coaxes more from him.

He stares across the harbour at the dozens of houses clinging to the steep hillside. Your house is up there, the one near the top with the small terraced garden and the shed leaning drunkenly against the rocky outcrop. He remembers looking up there before and seeing movement in the garden, the unmistakeable flitter of an excited child playing on his own. He knew even back then who the child was, of course, because he was the boy's godfather. But the child is gone now, and the garden is still. He shields his eyes to see whether you are sitting in the garden, staring down at him staring up. Perhaps you are, but it's too far to see. From this distance you'd simply fade into the background.

Leaving Jason, we rise up and revel in the sea breeze once again, like a seagull patrolling its familiar hunting ground. Jason continues stacking crates, and sometimes he thinks he'll soon be too old to carry on fishing the dawn. He has vague plans about opening a bed-and-breakfast somewhere inland, perhaps up on the moors where hikers hike all year round. He'll suggest it to your wife one day soon, and perhaps sometime—years from now, when Toby has been gone long enough for his shadow to disappear from the village—she will accept.

Following the stream inland, passing over the old slate roofs where seagulls roost, we spy the silvery snake of the stream passing beneath arched stone bridges and between buildings so tall and old they seem to lean in and touch. It looks serene and picturesque now, that stream, but in its bed it holds the silt of tragedy. Thirty years since the flood, but still it's talked about in Skentipple when the pubs are closing and old men and women are shadows in the narrow streets. Eight people washed away, and their names are immortalized in metal in the small village square. You never knew any of them—you were a child, and you lived a hundred miles away—but their names are still familiar to you.

We pass above the village's main car park, beyond which only people who live or work here are allowed to drive. The streets were never made for cars, and some of the sharper corners are carved with the memories of a thousand wing mirrors and bumpers. The car park is half empty today. Wendy sits on her usual bench, her old rucksack propped beside her and a plastic cider bottle already half empty between her knees. Her house is one of the finest in Skentipple, and also one of the largest, marking the entrance to the village from the main coastal road, but she has been like this ever since you can remember. She always dresses well and seems to take care of herself, but she won't let anyone close enough to tell for sure. No one can recall the last time anyone touched Wendy. She leaves money on shop counters and rarely waits for change, and this corner of the car park is her own.

Today, as every day, she's thinking about her husband Rodney and how he went away a decade before. And that is why there's no room in her life for anyone else, because she's doing her best to make Rodney still there. Her house echoes strangely at night, and every evening before bed she enters his study where she last saw him alive, and he is almost there again.

She looks up, as if she sees. But her expression does not change. She is long used to shadows in her life.

The road winds up from the car park, and on either side the valley slopes grow shallower. Most of the houses here are private, with a few holiday cottages scattered amongst them. We drift lower because there's something in the street, and we pass above a discarded toy propped in the gutter. It looks like a beanie doll, its brightly painted face faded a little by sunlight or rain, right leg missing. Such a shame.

We flit along with the wind, and then fall gently as a feather toward the Smugglers' Inn. It's an old pub built into the side of the valley, and Tony Fox the landlord once took you down into the basement to show you the start of the tunnel that leads all the way down to the sea. An old river course, he said, and you can remember the way the shadows shifted in there as his candle was kissed by a breeze, the rich smell of seaweed and rot even half a mile from the sea, and the sense of history stirring the old air. Untouched by sunlight, that place had little inkling that the world had moved on.

You asked Fox if he'd been all the way down, and he looked at you strangely, as if it was a stupid question. You still don't know.

Elizabeth is sitting in the small front beer

garden smoking a cigarette. She has taken up smoking again since Toby died, having given up years before when you started trying for a baby. You still remember her smile as she smoked her final cigarette and threw it away half-smoked. *Never again*, she said. *This is the first day of the future.*

Now, every day is the last day of the past.

Elizabeth is sad today, and she is always sad. You cannot know this, but you always assume it to be true. And you assume because you cannot bear the idea of her being happier than you. It was not her fault, and not yours either, but grief is a harsh mistress, and sometimes blame is the only way to appease her.

Your estranged wife enjoys this cigarette because it takes her back to a time of longing and hope. She doesn't think it's because it erases those smokeless years when everything was so happy—she's not certain that's the reason—but she allows herself to consider it. *Don't avoid thinking about him*, the doctor told her, and she has become adept at believing she's thinking about Toby without really considering him at all. Mostly she thinks about herself, as she was then. She closes her eyes and inhales again, and the smoke burns away the sweet smells of Skentipple. Maybe later she will see Jason, and his soft touch and restrained concern will further change her. Because that's what she is trying to do, and she can't help but acknowledge it. Change herself back to how she was before she met you, and before . . .

"Toby," she says, glancing up. A seagull cries out as it passes over the pub. Her heart misses a beat, and sometimes she hopes one of those missed beats will stretch and stretch until the next one is left waiting forever.

She closes her eyes, but does not see because we are not really here. She turns and goes back inside the pub—it's almost lunchtime, and soon she'll be cooking—and we are alone for a while at the top of the village, looking down the valley toward the blur of the sea.

Drifting back that way, something pulls us in. We feel the tug, though there is no urgency, and the air up here just feels so good and fresh. We're not part of the village or the air, but apart from them both.

Down in the street, the lost toy has vanished. Washed away by the rain, perhaps, like all those poor people three decades ago. But it has not rained for days.

And now there you are, sitting in your garden above the harbour looking down at the hypnotically shifting sea beyond the harbour wall. It sways and shifts, bulges and ebbs like the grey skin of a giant beast, a sleeping thing that has no concept of the humans who have come and built themselves around and over it. Sometimes there's a distant splash as a wave impacts the stone wall, and the sound serenades the gulls to provide a melody for the village.

You're motionless, because to move might allow in those memories you try so hard to keep at bay. You stare out and away from the garden where he played and laughed and ran, building sandcastles in his small sandpit, collecting bugs, pulling the petals from flowers to press, and sitting for long periods reading the books about pirates and smugglers he loved so much. And you keep your attention away from the house as well, though its stark south-facing wall reflects sunlight across you and provides a splash of warmth. In there he slept and cried and played, laughed and loved, and eventually died. In there you cannot bear to be, but the idea of leaving is even worse. Some of the villagers still ignore you because they don't know what to say.

But sometimes, walking through the village is the closest thing there is to an escape.

We can help. And then you, comforted and calm, may return the favour.

Though Ray had not spoken to his estranged wife for several months, somehow they had developed a routine. They had seen each other maybe half a dozen times, but even those brief sightings were at a distance, never close enough so they had to talk. They set Ray's heart skipping and his blood pulsing. Not because she was the woman he'd once loved—and who perhaps he still loved, if he could find the courage to look deep enough—but because from a distance, she reminded him so much of Toby.

Elizabeth had never told him why their life together had ended. Toby's death was not a reason, nor a cause. It had been a catalyst for something more, a distancing, a stretching of the love between them that had been fractured by their son's death, and eventually snapped. He often wondered whether it was because he reminded her of Toby as well. *He has your piercing blue eyes*, she used to say, Toby sleeping on his chest and her hair tickling his shoulder where she lay beside him. It's what had attracted her to Ray. The second thing she'd ever said to him was, *I always fancied Steve McQueen*. Neither could remember the first.

Skentipple was a small fishing village on Cornwall's south coast, and a place that lived two lives. One was an echo of every life lived there for hundreds of years—the trawlers went out with the tide, returned several hours later, and their catch was sold or auctioned off to provide a living for families whose ancestors had done the same. Fishermen were welcomed in by the pubs during the evenings, drinking local ale, singing, and telling stories of the sea whose origins were lost to the dark depths of time. Residents carried family names and traditions that were meaningless to outsiders, but which bore the substance of history to those who knew. Every building with its low doorways, every basement with a bricked-off section, every path that led up onto the cliffs or down to the rocky shore and then faded away . . . they all carried stories, and some were lost even to the memory of the village.

And the other life was more recent— the tourist's haven, catered for by the same pubs that entertained the fishermen. New restaurants, tea shops, and cafés that boasted local produce in their fresh cream cakes and crabmeat sandwiches. An element of the village's past had been eroded as surely as the cliffs it clung to, the abrasive rich families from London or the south-east who bought cottages to refurbish and rent to other strangers. They brought money and wonder to Skentipple, and when they wandered the narrow streets, alleys, and paths, some of them noticed the other people there: the villagers, breezing through ranks of tourists without a second glance as they went about their daily business. Two worlds in one, both of them overseen by the steep valley sides where people had deemed it necessary to build the most precarious dwellings.

Living in this place, avoiding someone was not easy. Though down at the harbour there was a network of alleys and paths, once away from the sea, there was only one road that led up out of the village, away from the restaurants, past the Smugglers' Inn, curving around old mad Wendy's house until it vented into the wild Cornish countryside. But Ray and

Elizabeth managed. She lived in a room above the Smugglers' Inn, and since she worked there as well, her visits to the harbour side were usually limited to evenings. Ray lived on the hillside above the harbour—he'd kept their family home because she couldn't, co-existing with memories she could not bear—and he usually visited the harbour during the day.

Evenings, he walked the cliffs.

Sometimes he wondered whether he should purposely try to bump into her. Talk, maybe even hold hands, and broach the subject of their loss as they should have a year before. Though he didn't think they had fallen out of love, he felt little for her anymore. Perhaps grief over Toby had eroded all capacity for other emotions, even love. But every time Ray thought of doing this, he considered the fact that *she* was not seeking *him* out, and illogical though it seemed, he took this as reason enough to maintain his routine.

Really, he was afraid.

But today was different. Today, he had

been sitting in the garden for hours, sleeping and waking, never quite sure whether he was dreaming of the village or seeing and hearing it for real. His hands and feet were cold from his long exposure to the autumn, and though he wore two woollen sweaters and a heavy coat, his sweat still managed to chill him. His limbs felt heavy and dead. The idea of a beer in one of the village pubs was attractive for once, and he left the house without checking the time. He had stopped wearing a watch months ago, tired of watching his life tick away.

Walking down the curving, steep path from his house toward the harbour, he passed an old woman on her way up. He'd never discovered her name, but they always exchanged a nod and a smile. Today she spoke, and Ray thought perhaps it was the first time.

"Love autumn," she said, panting. She was maybe eighty years old, and the steps and steep path up from the harbour were a challenge for Ray, someone half her age.

He was so surprised that he could not find

an answer.

"So how're you?" she asked.

"I'm . . ." *Terrible*, he thought. *I'm stuck a year ago.* "I'm not too bad," he said, and found a smile creeping across his face.

"Good to hear it," the woman said. She puffed a little, rubbing at her knees. "I'm always here. Well, nearly always. If you need me for anything."

"Thank you," Ray said. He knew her house, an old fisherman's cottage with its rough plaster walls inlaid with a beautiful array of shells. Toby had called it the shell house, and Ray remembered her talking to him once when he'd run on ahead. Ray and Elizabeth had climbed the hill to find their son accepting a slice of cake from the woman's withered hands. For them she'd only had a smile, but that had been enough to make them feel good.

She nodded and started past him, and Ray half turned on the narrow path.

"Really. Thank you."

"No need," she said, but her breath was

harsh now she was walking again. He watched her go, then turned and trotted down the steps to the wider path that led to the harbour.

This was the back end of Skentipple, the part where only the most adventurous tourists explored. There were no shops or cafés here, no pasty bakers or souvenir sellers, and it was rare that he saw anyone he didn't know walking this route. The path curved across the base of the hillside and opened up into the wide area around the harbour, and then he was among people.

As he walked, Ray had to force himself to look up from his shoes. He'd never understood where the shame of grief came from. At first it had been nervousness about people talking to him, and how they would deal with what had happened: some tried to act as if nothing had changed, and he hated that; others approached with sadness and uncertainty, and he hated that more. He'd soon come to realize that he preferred being left alone, and somehow and somewhere he'd managed to exude that desire. Occasionally he wondered what they thought of him now, but usually he didn't care. It was all part of blaming himself.

He walked around the harbour front, shops and pubs and cafés on his right, the harbour to his left. The tide was out with the boats, and the few crafts left were tilted over like one-legged men waiting to be lifted again. Dead fish silvered the silty bed, and seagulls strutted their stuff, taking their fill of the free meat. In one area, hundreds of crabs' claws lay half-buried where a crab fisherman tied his boat. The stream cut a path through the muddy bed, eventually joining the sea where it lapped at the harbour entrance.

Ray saw several people he knew. Max, the Weird Fish clothing shop owner, was taking in the jackets and sweaters he always hung across the outside of the shop's hoarding. He nodded once; Ray nodded and turned away. Next to Max's shop was the Seaview Café, and Muriel the owner sat outside, smoking. A huge mug of tea was on the table beside her, and from inside he heard some unidentifiable music rustling through the radio. Tourist season almost over, Muriel would adjust her opening times now to cater for the fishermen when they went out and came back in. She caught his eye and breathed out smoke, hiding behind it. *She's Elizabeth's*, Ray thought. He hated how what had happened to him and Elizabeth had polarized their friends.

"Afternoon, Muriel," he said as he passed by, not expecting or receiving an answer.

Jeff the seafood seller, his stall down on the harbour front where it had been for years. Franz the beachcomber, an old guy who lived a few miles inland, but who spent every Tuesday on Skentipple's small beach with his metal detector and rucksack. Where he spent the other days, Ray had never asked. Susan the barmaid. Philip, Pete, and other people, he knew them all but had stopped knowing them so well after Toby died. A few acknowledged him, and Franz tried briefly to engage him in conversation, but he always wanted to be somewhere else. Somewhere quieter. After staring at the sea for a few minutes—Toby haunting him with sandcastles and orange crab-fishing lines, calls for ice cream and startled giggles when the waves splashed him—he turned and started walking inland.

A few minutes later he saw Elizabeth. Just a flash of her hair to begin with, moving behind a window and lurking in the shadows beyond. He stood outside the Flag & Fisherman, a pub they had rarely frequented together because it was favoured by the younger generation from the village. Like every pub in Skentipple it possessed an undeniable aged charm, but went out of its way to advertise its large screen for viewing sporting events, and its three-pints-for-the-price-of-two happy hours. He frowned and tried to peer in the window. It *had* been her, he knew from the way his heart was thumping and a flush slowly faded across his face.

Pressing his face to the glass and shading his eyes, he scanned the pub's front bar. As he saw a youngster gesture to him and say something to his laughing friend, Elizabeth's face became clear to him. She was sitting by the old fireplace, slouched back on a bench with a large glass of wine on the table on front of her. Beside her sat Jason, the fisherman, his old friend. His large weathered hand rested on her leg, and she was leaning into his shoulder, laughing at something he was still saying. His lips moved soundlessly, Ray's ex-wife's shoulders shook, and she found humour in Jason's company.

Ray wondered how many glasses of wine she'd had before this one. He'd tried turning to drink, but found that it only brought Toby's memories closer to him, and changed his dreams into nightmares that lingered through the following day's hangover. He had no idea whether Elizabeth had resorted to alcohol. She'd never been a big drinker before, but losing Toby had made new people of them both.

He stayed there for a few panicked seconds,

angry at Jason—who had once been his friend, lost now in the same casual way as his wife— and raging at Elizabeth. When she looked up and saw him, her expression changed into something awful. The laughter faded, leaving behind a painted-on smile, and she seemed to *pause*, growing so motionless that she was his only focus, and the rest of the world orbited around her. Then her mouth fell open. Ray did not hear the name that tumbled out.

Making his way back across the harbour toward the hillside, he tried to understand why he felt so angry. He'd known about Jason and Elizabeth for a couple of months. But this was the first time he'd seen them together. And as he climbed the steps and steep paths toward his house, he came to realize what troubled him so much. It wasn't Jason's big hand on her thigh, with all of its implications, and it wasn't the fact that she appeared so at ease with another man. It wasn't even his mumbled comments and her easy laughter.

It was the idea that Elizabeth was moving

on. She had left him alone out in the street, and after what they had been through, she could still find it in herself to laugh.

By the time he reached his house, he was crying. And by the time he'd managed to unlock the door, fall inside and slam it behind him, he knew what he had to do.

2

We rise from the sad house with the crying man and submit to the breeze, now carrying the growing chill of dusk. The sun is setting behind the opposite valley ridge, silhouetting the sparse trees growing up there in defiance of the storms that sweep this coast. They throw long shadows out across the valley, and if the confusion of buildings and water was not so extreme, they might even be visible down there. But street lights are flickering on to kill the shadows, and windows throughout the village are illuminated from within.

Up to the ridge and along from the village, and a fox gambols on the slope of bracken and ferns leading to the sheer cliffs. Several shapes play around it, but they're too quick and shy to manifest properly. The wild welcomes the dusk, as it has since the advent of humanity. People have taken the day for themselves, putting limits on it, sectioning it, adjusting it for their own means and ends. But nighttime, an absence, still belongs to the land.

Yet there are those who walk the night. People who tread carefully, but relish the freedom inherent in the dark winds. Their minds are often closer to the nature of things, or the nature *in* things, and they understand more than most that the wild is a cycle like everything else. There are the aeons, and the ages, the years and the seasons, but there is also day and night, and there lies the truest of nature's distinctions.

The cliff path is deserted tonight, swept of fallen leaves by the sea breeze. The hawthorn trees on either side are mostly leafless now, and the ferns are fading to brown, readying to die back and give way to new growth in several months' time. Some life hibernates over seasons, and some hides for much shorter periods.

Below, down through the thick ferns and gorse, clinging to the edge of the cliff like a huge barnacle, we see the old stone structure. Forever, it has been a forgotten remnant of the village's past. Perhaps a lookout post for fishermen, or a refuge of some sort. Maybe it is even a folly, built by a rich villager of yesteryear to a love that might or might not have been his. There is little vandalism here. None of the casual spraypainted exhortations of youths, or the intentional removal of blocks to tumble over the cliff, whose sheer edge is only a few short steps away. It could be that kids don't know about it, or maybe there are other reasons. Perhaps animals use it for a shelter sometimes, but today . . .

There's a spread of things outside the small building's seaward opening, and from inside . . . is that a light? Faint, a feeble glow like the echo of the sun's setting beams that to most would not even be visible.

And here we are: sitting in the doorway is a man, where perhaps he wasn't before.

He's an old man. He's smoking a pipe, and its intermittent glow gives him a lighthouse face. Something sways in his hand as he works his fingers. He stretches, and feels the bones in his shoulder grate together. The first sign of age. Many other aches and pain have developed since then, but these are still the worst. At least his fingers can still flex, and his hands still grip, and at least his sight is still sharp.

The shape in his hand is an old beanie doll, and tonight he will give it a new leg.

He stopped crying before he opened the door, because he had spilled enough tears in that room.

Ray had used to read a lot of fiction. But since Toby had passed away, what reading he did usually revolved around real life, and was lighter. Sports commentaries, biographies, humorous books . . . fiction was inevitably about conflict and loss, and his life had suffered enough of those for real. He couldn't lose himself anymore. His disbelief could no longer be suspended, because he was always in the here and now. But when he'd used to read, one of the things he'd scoffed at was some people's approach to bereavement. *The room was exactly the same as the day his wife was murdered*, a line in a book would say, and Ray would joke about it to Elizabeth. He'd tell her that when *she* was murdered he'd clear their room out straight away, move to the spare room, and take in a lodger. A pair of Swedish au pairs, he'd suggested one day, to his wife's strained laughter. Back then he had demanded that his fiction be realistic—truth in lies—and he could not imagine anyone handling loss in that way. It was the clichéd idea of being stuck in the moment, and not moving on.

Ray rested his hand on Toby's bedroom door, readying himself for what he would see. The room beyond was not as it had been on the day Toby died. He was not in it, for a start, motionless and cold in his bed, waiting to be found by his adoring parents, who couldn't understand why he was still asleep—they'd never had to wake him before; he was always up before them, ready to poke them in the ear and force them to rise . . .

The bed was stripped now, all the bedding discarded. Elizabeth had bought a load of new bedding, but left it on the old mattress in its packets, never to be made. Later, after she left, Ray had spread blankets across the mattress to hide as much as he could, but still had not made the bed properly. That would be like waiting for someone else to come.

"Rise and shine, Tobes," he said, pushing the door open. The room smelled of dust and damp—there was a problem with the old stone walling in one corner, something their local builder had never been able to solve. The curtains were permanently open, the view out onto the dusky garden obscured only by glass that desperately needed cleaning.

He still came in here sometimes. It wasn't a shrine or anything; he'd tried many times to convince himself of that. There were a couple of boxes of books that he'd packed away, stacked in one corner and still awaiting their trip to the charity shop. A pair of folded curtains were dropped casually on the floor in one corner. It wasn't a bedroom anymore, but it was still Toby's room. That was for sure. He felt his son in here, and as he knelt by the bed, he experienced a shattering flashback.

The worst memories were those he thought he'd forgotten.

He and Toby kneel by the bed because his son has been taught how to pray in school. Ray's not comfortable with this. *I don't want him force-fed and brainwashed*, he'd said. But Elizabeth had calmed his anger. *We were. We made up our own minds.* So just for that evening Ray kneels with his son, and smiles when the boy makes up his own prayers. *Thank God for Mummy and Daddy, and the sea, and chocolate ice cream, and the Power Rangers, the film not the telly program. Thank God for pancakes and Mars Bars, and crisps, and curry, and . . .* He frowns, glancing sidelong at Ray to make sure he has his eyes closed.

Dad!

Sorry, son. Carry on.

Thank God for food and drink, and stuff. Oh, and for Jesus Christ. Amen. He glances up at Ray. *The man in the collar said God knew his son was going to die. Why did he let that happen?*

It's just a story, son. Made up. Like Aesop's Fables, only not as good.

Okay. Dad, my Ben 10 watch is broken.

Ray squeezed his lips tight at the memory, and frowned. Had he ever fixed that watch? Had he? He remembered telling Toby he'd look at it, that maybe the batteries had run out, but he couldn't recall ever hearing its strange distorted sound again, nor seeing its glow on his son's wrist.

He reached under the bed. There was a plastic box under there where he'd stored a load of Toby's toys, and as he pulled it out, he knew he was about to be assailed by memories. The blue click-on lid was covered with dust.

Removing the lid, he leaned it against the bed and just stared. Inside the box was a riot of colours and shapes, toys he remembered

38

and some he did not. Action figures pointed weapons at him, remote controlled cars sat motionless, cuddly toys huddled together in the box's corners. He moved some toys aside and something growled.

Ray gasped and sat back, listening to the noise. He remembered it, a long low growl that emanated from an alligator with a man's body. He couldn't recall which TV program or comic it came from, but he pictured Toby sitting on their living room floor with this and other figures, indulging in some unreachable battle or scenario expressed through sound and movement. Most of it took place in his head, and that was gone now. When he was alive, memories of those battles would have existed somewhere in his child's brain. But now those conflicts could never exist again.

The alligator fell silent and Ray delved farther into the box. He was sad, but the familiar crippling grief remained at bay. The toys felt good in his hands. Some of them he put in a pile on the carpet; others—mostly action figures—he stood in uneven ranks on the bed, like startled mercenaries brought out of retirement. They'd been in hiding for almost a year, and now they were exposed once again, but this time there would be no play.

They were being sorted out. It wasn't just this box under the bed; there were toys and books everywhere. The top of the wardrobe was stacked with board games. Another box at the foot of the bed held thousands of building blocks and associated pieces—boards, ties, small motors, wheels, batteries. A book case beside the door was home to over a hundred books, ranging from the first cloth book they'd bought Toby as a baby, through picture and pop-up books they'd read to him when very young, to volumes he'd started to read himself. There was a book about a talking dragon, and one about a boy who tried to catch a star. He'd been a good reader, one of the best in his school class.

There were a few books that were too old

for him, but which Ray hadn't been able to resist buying. He paused, staring at these, because Toby would never know their stories. He might have looked at them—he'd liked to fan pages and scan pictures—but their uniqueness would never be known to him, and that brought on Ray's first tear since entering the room.

"No," he said. "Not now. Not yet." He tipped the plastic box, spilling toys across the floor. Something bounced from his leg, and he froze. There was the Ben 10 watch that had broken. He picked it up and turned it in his hand, looking for the battery compartment. The battery was still inside. He turned the dial that exposed different monsters, snapped the front of the watch shut, and a small spring tumbled out.

Ray couldn't see where the missing part had come from, but guessed it was the reason the watch no longer worked. It was supposed to light up and make a noise, but now it was just a lump of plastic . . . a lump of useless plastic, pointless, and—

He stood and was about to throw the thing against the wall, but then paused. The toys on the bed watched him, and he went from one to the next, checking each until he found what was wrong. With some it was obvious—a missing arm, a torn joint, a crushed head. With others, the fault was not so noticeable, but he always found it.

Every toy was broken. Ray frowned, clutching the Ben 10 watch and trying to remember when they'd all been consigned to the box beneath the bed. He'd thought it was after they lost Toby, but now he wasn't so sure. Now, he seemed to remember piling all those broken toys in there himself, and there had likely been an empty promise to his son that he would fix them all soon.

But he never had mended the broken watch.

"Damn it," Ray said softly, gathering the toys from the floor and adding them to those on the bed. He made sure they were spread evenly, none of them hiding another, because they each deserved his attention. A year ago, two, three, he should have given them his attention then. But other things had conspired, more urgent matters like what they'd have for dinner, the latest bill that needed paying, which movie he and Elizabeth would watch when Toby had been tucked up in bed. . . .

"Sorry, Toby," he said. "Really, son, I'm so sorry." He'd been a terrible father. He hadn't deserved such a wonderful boy. People would judge him and he wanted that, because he was so unable to judge himself. All these thoughts harried at him, though he knew none of them were completely true.

Grabbing the Ben 10 watch, he turned from the room, shutting off the light behind him and closing the door.

Standing on the landing, Ray heard raindrops tapping at the window. They were blown by a strengthening sea breeze. He took a deep breath and thought of the cliff top, how wild and untouched it was up there, and how alone he would be.

The broken toy went into his coat pocket, and five minutes later he was making his way up the coastal path toward the cliffs.

The storm's growth tracked his progress up out of Skentipple. When he left his home, the rain was light, the wind gentle but starting to gust harder. The coastal path curved up and out of the village, and the higher he walked, the stronger the wind and more persistent the rain. It was as if the weather sensed the village held some semblance of civilization, and that the cliffs were the wilds.

Ray loved walking up here. Being alone was part of it, because circumstance had made him the loner he'd always believed he was meant to be. But there was also an element of feeling closer to Toby here than anywhere, even in his home. The little boy had loved walking, adored the views, had been fascinated by nature and the wildness of that place. It had started as a toddler's eternal interest in somewhere new, but by the time he died, Toby's love of nature was becoming obvious. Like most kids, he was drawn to dinosaurs and the strange mysteries they represented—monsters in a world where adults said there were none—but animals he could see, hear, and sometimes touch had always held greater allure for him.

Once, they had found a dead seagull tucked beneath a huge sprout of ferns. It had taken Ray a couple of minutes to approach, because there had been no obvious injuries. He'd seen the birds close up many times before—troubling holidaymakers for food, or crying out when their eggs had been holed in the annual cull—and he had always respected their size and aggression. But like any living thing of any size, seeing it motionless looked so wrong. There was something unearthly about a creature that should be revelling in movement being so still. He'd edged closer, reaching out his hand, Toby hanging onto his leg not in fear, but for comfort because his father was there with him. And just before he'd touched the bird, Ray thought he saw it move. But it was only an errant breeze twitching one of its complex, beautiful feathers.

Toby had looked the same that morning when they found him. Motionless, silent, not there. He'd worn the features of their son, but he had never been so still.

And there were so many things to collect, so many of nature's wonders to marvel over or question, especially when you viewed the world from a child's eyes. Toby had seen so much that Ray had always taken for granted, and Ray had been forced to buy several books just so he could keep up with his son's demand for information. Plants and flowers needed categorizing and pressing, and Ray had made a small book-sized flower press for his boy. Small mammals needed naming, their tracks identifying, habitats understanding. Ray had learned at the same time as Toby that there were shrews, badgers, rabbits, stoats, rats, voles, moles, hedgehogs, foxes, and perhaps even deer living on the stretch of wild countryside above the village. There were birds to watch through binoculars, species identified by their type of flight or song, and the two of them had often spent hours sitting up there watching birds fishing, or dropping shells onto rocks to break them open. It had become a revelation for Ray, and in some ways he'd found himself more surprised at the variety of wildlife around them than Toby.

Because Toby was a little boy who *expected* amazing things. His mind was wide open and prepared for there to be a multitude of discoveries yet to make. His sense of wonder had been alive and on fire, and Ray's . . . perhaps that had dwindled and died with the withering effects of age. He'd often watch his son stop to root through undergrowth or examine a caterpillar beneath a magnifying glass, and grow sad at the idea that wonder was such a difficult commodity to retain. More often than not he would have simply walked on.

Elizabeth used to complain when the two

of them embarked on their expeditions during bad weather. *But Mummy*, Toby would wail, *some of the animals only come out of their houses when they know there's no one there*. It was an incredibly mature observation for someone so young—he was acknowledging that the world existed without him, as well as with him—and Elizabeth had never complained again.

With Toby, he had never been scared. But now he felt the wild inside him, not just all around. The cliff path at night was an alien place to Ray, one where his son no longer existed, shadows throbbed with malice, and memories flitted through the darkness like teasing ghosts.

He paused and turned around, looking back the way he had come. He could still see a few of Skentipple's more remote buildings, but most of the village was hidden from view behind the shoulder of the land. It was built in an inlet in the coast, a natural harbour protected from the sea by the high cliffs on either side, and from here he could see little more than its glow. Rain falling over Skentipple was set aflame by the lights, and it seemed that huge fires danced in the air.

Elizabeth was down there somewhere. Still in the Flag and Fisherman perhaps, several drinks in and relaxing more in Jason's company. His hand might be higher up her thigh now, little finger nestling against the place only Ray had seen and touched and tasted for the last ten years. He wondered what she thought of as she drank and laughed at the big fisherman's jokes, whether she sometimes saw Toby watching her through the dusty windows, or heard him asking her what she was doing. Ray had never actually seen or heard his dead son, but he felt his presence everywhere. *It's your memories where he's still alive*, someone had told him shortly after his little boy's cremation. He couldn't even recall who she had been. An aunty, perhaps, or one of Elizabeth's friends. Ray had been experiencing a moment of sheer panic at what they had done, destroying what little was left of Toby, and he had tortured himself for not burying the boy and allowing him the chance to fade. *That wasn't really him*, the woman had said, and she had touched Ray's forehead, thumb reaching down to smudge his tears. *This is the place where he still lives.*

Not in Heaven, Ray had said, but it had not been a question. Then, and ever since, he had coveted the comfort that faith gave some people, but it had never been a part of him. *It's just a story, son*, he'd told Toby. *Made up.*

Sometimes he thought about Toby's last moments, and what he had been dreaming when he died.

He turned away from the village and continued walking. He wanted to go far enough to leave its glow behind, to a place where the only light was the occasional glimpse of the half-moon through storm clouds, speckling the wet ground in a million places and glancing from the wild waves. The ground was wet, and slippery in places where the bare path had turned muddy. This route was used extensively during tourist season, but now that the year's end loomed, it was only the occasional hardy local who came this way, walking their dog or their lover or themselves. To his right lay the cliff's edge, farther down the slope and shielded from him by growths of low hawthorn bushes, brambles, and the remnants of the summer's ferns. He knew if he worked his way down lesser-trodden paths, he would draw much closer to the cliff, but he was mostly safe where he walked now.

A gust of wind brought the scents of the sea, and rain stung the right side of his face. He heard a cough, and cleared his throat before realizing the sound had not come from him.

Ray paused, motionless beneath the weather doing its best to set him tumbling, or rolling, or rushing back for shelter. A chill ran down his back like a drip of icy water, and he squinted as he scanned the path ahead of him. A dozen steps from where he stood, slightly uphill, a holly tree leaned toward the sea, and he remembered that directly beyond it the path veered left and down a short series of uneven, naturally formed steps. A shadow stood beneath that tree now, so still he wondered whether it was his own. But the moon was to his right, not behind him. And then the shape dropped away along the path.

"Hey!" Ray called, because the complicit storm of rain and wind needed breaking. He stumbled ahead, slipping and almost sprawling in the mud, heart thudding and chest pulsing from the shock. When he found his feet again and paused beneath the holly, the path ahead and below him appeared empty. He moved on, stepping carefully down the rocky steps. Movement ahead drew his attention again, and as he glanced up, his foot slipped. He reached out and grasped a branch hanging above him, howling as several leaf spikes pierced his palm and fingers.

The shadow moved along the path and then paused again, as if drawing him on.

Ray let go of the branch and put his hand to his mouth. He tasted blood. *It doesn't matter,* he thought. *Even if it is someone, I don't need to meet them.* But something about the vague form lured him on, and he followed.

He passed by several places that held memories of Toby, but kept his eyes on the figure. It maintained the same distance between them, however fast or slow Ray moved. Once, he started running along a stretch of path he knew to be relatively level and unhindered by protruding stones or roots. The shadow also ran.

At last he paused, examining his still-bleeding hand in the moonlight. Rain diluted the blood and swilled it across his palm and wrist, inside the arm of his coat to stain the fabric in there.

"Fuck you!" he shouted into the storm, and he turned around to walk back the way he had come. At home he'd build the first fire of the winter, lock all the doors, close the curtains, and his house would become his castle against the world. He would open a bottle of wine— just for a glass or two, because drinking never numbed the pain—and listen to the storm defeated against the walls. If memories came to haunt, so be it. If tears came, he would let them flow. But he could rest with the knowledge that he'd at least commenced clearing Toby's room. Over the next few days the room would change, and as it became a spare room for visitors that never came, so he too would try to move on. He'd always hated symbolism—he prided himself on his straight thinking—but sometimes, since Toby's death, it was the only way he could see things.

"Have you brought me a broken toy?" a voice said.

Ray spun around. An old man stood several feet from him along the path. His voice had carried well, though he'd spoken softly.

"Who . . . who are you?"

"Just an old man." He eyed Ray up and down, expression neutral. He wore a long black raincoat with a hood pulled over his head, and he stood leaning forward slightly, right hand propped against his right knee. It was a calm pose, as opposed to a frail one.

"What toy?" Ray asked. *How did he know? What was this?* He brushed his hand across his coat, feeling the uneven shape of the Ben 10 watch in his pocket.

The old man blinked, and water gathered on his long eyelashes.

Ray took a step forward to see the man clearer. It was an unconscious decision, and as his foot lifted and moved forward, he was assaulted by a flood of thoughts: *stupid move, show him I'm not scared, he'll be startled, who is he, what's he doing up here, he knows about the toy but he can't, so he doesn't he doesn't know, and I'm going closer even though—*

"Who are you?" Ray asked again as his foot hit the ground, and the man took a hasty step backward. His eyes grew wider, and he stood up straight. For the first time Ray noticed the walking stick, and the way the man's pale hand was gripped around the handle. But something about his expression was false. It wasn't quite a smile he wore, but it didn't quite vanish, either.

"Told you, boy. Just an old man."

"Out in this storm?"

"So you going to give me the toy?"

"I don't recognize you from Skentipple."

"I don't live down in the village," the old man said. "Go there sometimes, but got no need to live there." The wind continued to blow, and rain hushed down all around them, but the conversation was clear on both sides. Ray had to raise his voice, but the man seemed unconcerned.

"So where do you live?"

"Near enough." He looked Ray up and down again, his gaze finally settling on the coat pocket.

"I've got no toy," Ray said, harsher than he'd intended.

The man seemed to lose interest, turning to look out to sea at where a ship's lights blinked on the horizon. He transferred his walking stick from his left hand to his right, and reached up to scratch his scalp. The movement lifted the hood and, facing the moon, Ray saw his face for the first time. He was extremely old, skin creased and sagging from his face. His eyes were wide and intelligent, but gravity and time had pulled down the flesh around them, giving him a permanently sad expression. A few wisps of grey hair protruded from the hood, and his chin and cheeks were white with stubble. His jaw was strong, and Ray knew for sure that he still had his own teeth.

"You should be getting home, then," the man said. "No need to be out on a night like this when there's sorting to be done."

"Did you walk from along the cliffs?" Ray asked, nodding past the old man. It was at least three miles to the next small village, up and down treacherous and challenging paths even in bright sunlight.

"No, son," the old man said. "And . . . really, I can mend it. You want me to. It'll help."

"I told you, I don't have a fucking toy for you to fix! What is it with you? Don't you just—" A more violent gust of wind roared in, forcing rain almost horizontally before it, and Ray turned from the sea. The rain struck his back hard as driven hail, and when the gust died down and he turned back to the old man, he was just as he'd been before. Hood pulled forward a little more, perhaps. Leaning a little heavier on his cane. Ray didn't think for a moment that the man hadn't felt the gust, but he seemed completely unbothered by it.

"Just keeping a promise will set you free," the old man said, and yet again his voice carried through the storm. "Well, if you're not me, that is." Then he turned and walked back along the path.

For a moment Ray considered going after him, but what could he really gain? The guy was obviously on another planet. He felt a moment of concern and responsibility—the old fool was walking along the cliffs, farther into the wild, and the storm was gathering strength—but he'd said he didn't come from the village anyway. Maybe he had a shack out there somewhere, or a little hut hidden up on the moors. Even though Ray and Elizabeth had lived here for ten years, they were still considered newcomers by some of Skentipple's oldest families, and perhaps this man was a village secret.

Ray ducked from another withering blast of wind and rain, and when he looked again, the man was gone. No shadow, no sign of movement. But Ray was not that mad, nor that far gone. He *had* talked to an old man up on this cliff, and that old man—

He had known about the broken watch.

"Damn it," Ray muttered, rain running down his face and onto his lips. It tasted of the sea. His hand still stung from the thorns, as if reminding him that it had been hurt as well, and he tried to examine the wounds in the moonlight. But he could not focus. He kept glancing around at shadows threatening to crowd in. Far out to sea, lightning stabbed the horizon.

He started back toward the village, moving quickly along the dark path. The moon had retreated fully behind the clouds now, and the only trace of illumination came from the reflected glow from the clouds' underside. Skentipple's borrowed light guided him in. He slipped several times, but managed to remain standing. Water flowed across the path on its journey toward the cliff edge, and he wondered what would happen if he submitted to that flow.

After Toby died, Ray had considered suicide three times. Once he'd gone so far as to walk up here to the cliff top and explore a less-trodden path, one that led down past an old stone bench buried deep beneath a bramble bush and skirted close to the cliff edge. He'd stood on that path for some time, the ground ending maybe ten steps in front of him, and all he'd needed to do was force his way through the twisted heathers and gorse that grew to the edge. That had been three months after Toby died, and three days after Elizabeth moved out. He'd stood there, analyzing in a dispassionate, objective way his reasons for wanting to die. And much as the world without his son was a terrible, empty place, he hated the trace of self-pity he could not help feeling. If he fell, it was Elizabeth he'd be thinking of, and how she would react to his death.

He'd sighed, and then glanced left along the cliff. Just in view was the regular edge of a stone wall. It was closer to the cliff's edge than him, and he'd leaned forward trying to make out exactly what it was. A building of some kind, he thought. A small hut, maybe, buried by plant growth, surely never used. He'd wondered at someone loving this view so much that they'd gone to the effort of constructing something up here. And then he'd sat there for a long time, listening to the sea, smelling gorse, feeling the gentle warm breeze against his face. . . .

It took twenty minutes to get back to the village, and by the time he reached his home, his limbs were shaking with exertion. His clothes were sodden and heavy, and the final climb up the paths and steps to his front door almost defeated him. But he made it inside, hiding from the storm and drawing curtains against the cheery lights of the village.

He set the open fire in the living room, and as the rolled newspaper burned and the wood caught, he stripped. The warmth from the fire was almost instantaneous. He unfolded a rack and hung his clothes, then remembered the Ben 10 watch.

Have you brought me a broken toy?

It wasn't in any of his coat pockets. Ray searched again, making sure he checked each pocket thoroughly. Then, naked, he went through the kitchen to the back door, turning on all the lights and looking on the floor. There was no sign of it.

So you going to give me the toy?

He went back to the living room and checked the coat again, then his trouser pockets, then retraced his steps to the back door one more time. He flicked on the outside light and opened the door, forgetting his nakedness as he went out beneath the small porch and scanned the broken stone path leading to the small garden gate.

The watch was gone. He'd dropped it. *I have to go and find it*, he thought, but the storm had reached its full fury now, and Ray suddenly felt more weary than he'd realized. He shut the back door and checked the kitchen clock.

It was almost midnight. He'd been up on the cliffs for two hours.

"Tomorrow," he said to the terrible empty house. "I'll go and find it tomorrow."

He dragged a duvet down from upstairs and curled up on the sofa, staring into the flames as the coals caught. *There are caves in there!* Toby used to shout as he watched the fire, and Ray saw them now, bright glowing caves inhabited by fantastic creatures and a child's innocent hopes.

3

We drift through the storm where no bird dares fly. The sense of being alone is staggering; there are no contrasts between up and down, here and there. Wind surges like angry breaths of forgotten gods, and rain lances through the air. Lightning bursts all around—the gods' fury given form—and the world shakes.

Down, floating down onto the village, the life to be witnessed past midnight is different from that during daylight hours. Descending over the full harbour and past seagull shit-streaked rooftops, an old man walks through the warren of streets and alleys. He is making his sad way home after several pints at the Flag & Fisherman. Twenty years ago he went out on a fishing boat with five of his mates, and he was the only one to return. He still dreams of them, especially his brother's face as the sea took him down, and sometimes in those dreams he remembers other things in the water with them that day. Amorphous, amorous things, waving hair and smooth skin, claws and the insinuation of sharp, shark-like teeth. His name is Duncan, and he can still remember the day they found his friend David's body. Drowned, the doctors said when they opened him up, but there was no mention of the other wounds on his corpse. No one even seems to remember those other wounds. Duncan drinks alone most nights now, and he knows that many in the village think him mad. He walks home in the darkness, still scared of what the storm might contain.

As we move away from Duncan, he pauses in the street and looks up into the storm. There's nothing to see, but still he staggers sideways and leans against a wall. Perhaps madmen can see farther.

We peer down into a small, overgrown garden, where two teenagers on their way home from the pub are rutting. She's called Maxine, and as she bends over she clasps her knickers, worried that they'll drop and get dirty and her mother will see. She's soaking and cold from the rain, but hot inside. The boy's name is Flynn. His family has lived in the village forever, and he has some vague idea that he and Maxine might be distant cousins somewhere down the line, but she has a sweet arse and cute tits. He looks around warily, worried about getting caught and eager to get it over with, but he's had too much to drink, and this might take a while. When he's older he'll think back to this moment as the time his life changed, because he's not using a condom and Maxine isn't on the pill, and lightning thrashes in a new life.

Beyond the young lovers, giving them their privacy, the house is not too far away. It's an old rundown place, great swathes of cement render crumbled from the outside walls by frost. Rachel does her best, but with Johnny run away to Bodmin with that slut Lucy-Anne Woodhams, she's left here with Ollie, a house that needs maintaining, and two jobs. She can only do so much. She's sitting in

Ollie's room, the curtains drawn against the storm, a tumbler of whiskey in her hand, legs drawn up under her on the large wicker chair. Ollie is sleeping contentedly in his bed, and Rachel is confused. Her boy has been sick for several weeks now, and the doctors have given her varying diagnoses. Her GP told her that it was tonsillitis, and that sometimes young lads like Ollie can suffer from it badly: fever, terrible sore throat, swollen tongue, vomiting, breathing difficulties. She's been to hospital with him twice, and the tests have come back indicating he has glandular fever. That worries Rachel, because she had that illness when she was young and its regular recurrence is one of the main things she remembers from her teens. Whatever is wrong with him, Ollie has been home from school for three weeks, meaning that her working patterns at the bakery during the day have been haphazard at best. Margaret the owner is sympathetic, but she's also said she might have to let Rachel go and have her niece Maxine work the still-busy lunchtime shift. She doesn't pay much, and if Rachel hired a babysitter to come and look after Ollie for those four hours, she'd end up working them for a little over ten pounds. It's a problem—so much so that for the last three days she's been considering contacting that fucking bastard Johnny and begging him for help. But this evening Ollie seemed to suddenly improve, between the time she started dinner and the time they'd finished. His pallor lifted, his eyes grew bright again, his colour returned, and by nine o'clock he wanted to go out for ice cream. If there'd been one place in the village still open at that time, she'd have gone out to buy him a whole tub.

So she sits watching him now, and the frown is only a little to do with the mystery of his miraculous recovery. Mostly it's because he is cuddling his old beanie doll, and she disposed of Oswald a few weeks ago when its leg came off and started leaking bean-innards. Now it's whole again, and so, it seems, is Ollie.

We move away from Rachel now, back into the storm, because come morning she will have forgotten Oswald and found a measure of happiness again. On to the top of the village, following the direction of the storm, and in a small attic room above the Smugglers' Inn, a man and woman sleep wrapped together, naked, warm. There are dreams in this room, and Elizabeth opens her eyes and cries out as she hears her dead son's laughter. The fisherman, Jason, mumbles something in his sleep and cups her breast, and Elizabeth lifts her head and stares through the curtainless window at the storm beyond. She's breathing heavily, and soon the tears on her face echo the raindrops on glass.

Back through the village, its secret lives huddled down against the storm, we see and sense other people enjoying or suffering different dreams. There is laughter and sadness, lovemaking and lovelessness. And up past the last of the houses, on the cliffs overlooking the sea, here he is, the man sitting in a small stone shelter working by the light of a fire.

"Wake up, sleepy bum!" Toby shouted, and Ray smiled as he surfaced from sleep. He could smell fire, and they were camping on the moors, one of their neighbours having already fired up the barbeque for breakfast. "Sleepy bum, sleepy bum!" Toby called, and Ray was stiff and sore. *I just love my home comforts*, he remembered Elizabeth saying about her ambivalence toward camping, but this holiday would change that.

Ray opened his eyes, expecting to see Toby kneeling just outside their tent compartment, ready to open the zip and leap onto their airbed. But everything was wrong. The ceiling was too high, and lined with spider webs. The airbed was harder than it should have been, and he wondered whether it had gone down during the night.

Reality crowded in and Ray groaned. The

smell of smoke remained.

He sat up slowly. Some of the duvet had slipped from the sofa during the night, and he was cold. He'd gone to sleep still naked, the fire roaring in the hearth, but now it was a sculpture of ash, and he saw his breath condensing before him.

"Damn it, Toby," Ray whispered, as if his son really had woken him. He stood and walked slowly to the kitchen, pausing with every step to twist and turn the kinks from his limbs and back. He must have slept in the same position all night, and now his body wanted to remain in that shape. He was like the teenager Toby had never become, annoyed at being woken up, eager to remain exactly where he was because nothing outside could possibly be of any interest. Ray had often dwelled upon how the future would have played out, and what sort of a teenager Toby would've been. He himself had been a bit sulky and shy, but he'd never given his parents anything to really worry about. He'd been a virgin until nineteen, so there had never been girl issues, only no-girl issues. No drugs, only booze. Ray had always hoped Toby would be as easy to handle, but only in his darkest moments had he ever considered his son no longer being there at all.

In the kitchen, he slipped on his wet walking boots from the previous night and padded across the slate floor to the sink. Filling the kettle, he looked out on the little garden. Puddles of muddy water lay where he'd once planned a small vegetable patch. Leaves had been blown against the rocky slope that formed the garden's rear perimeter, sticking there in the wet. The fence, always rickety, now leaned at almost forty-five degrees. He'd have to fix that before the next storm came in, otherwise—

He remembered the old man, the things he'd said, and in the daylight they seemed . . . if not ridiculous, then distant. Unlikely.

"Weird old coot," he muttered. He crossed to the fridge, and it was only as he passed the glazed back door that he remembered his nakedness. He glanced out, across the garden at the path that climbed past the house, thinking, *Of course there'll be no one there, it's early, and it's my house anyway, whose business is it if—*

The old woman from the shell house was standing out on the path, head tilted back as she laughed at the sky. If he'd opened the door he'd have heard her cackling. Ray quickly covered his crotch with his left hand. The woman continued down the path smiling and shaking her head, and then he heard the muffled crackle and buzz of the Ben 10 watch.

He froze, watching the old woman turn left and start descending the old stone steps.

The watch sounded again, as if someone had twisted the face and then slammed it shut on a new monster. That sound had driven him mad on Toby's fifth birthday, for some reason more than all the other beeps, shrieks and whistles that seemed to emanate from every modern kid's toys. But of course, the watch had broken. And he'd put it away in that box beneath the bed, promising his son he'd fix it and make it well again.

Like any kid, Toby had quickly moved on to something else.

Ray turned around and scanned the kitchen. Maybe it was still in his coat pocket, and the rain had got in and shorted a broken circuit or—

It buzzed again and he turned back to the door. It was lying on the step outside—the step wet, the watch completely dry. Ray unlocked the door, glancing around quickly to make sure no one else would get an eyeful today, and then squatted to pick it up. He hesitated just for a second, hand an inch away from the watch. *I searched for it, must have dropped it, and now* . . . He picked it up and went back inside, moving through to the hallway and climbing the dogleg staircase.

He sat on his bed and stared at the toy. Shook it. Looked for water droplets, any sign that it had spent the night exposed to the elements. But it was completely dry. He lifted the face, turned the dial until another monster was illuminated, then closed it again.

Maybe the old woman had found it and dropped it on his step. That would explain what she'd been doing there. But she'd been walking down the path from her own home when he'd seen her, not leaving his small sloping garden. *And it was broken. The spring fell out. It was incomplete when I lost it, and now . . .*

"Now it's complete again."

And because there was no explanation that made sense, he took the toy back into Toby's room and left it for a while.

Washing and dressing, he concentrated on shaving, the bathroom's décor, flossing, brushing his hair, what he might have for breakfast, what he'd need to fix the fence later that day, and all the while that broken thing was on his mind, fixed now and in the next room.

Standing on the landing, facing the open door to Toby's old room, Ray felt more normal and *there* than he had since waking. *I dropped it, someone found it and fixed it and brought it back for me,* he thought. *Or maybe when it dropped from my pocket, it hit the ground, dislodged something that was . . .*

But there was the spring that had fallen from the toy. And when he'd started back down the cliff path after leaving the old man, he'd felt the lump in his coat, touching it protectively because it was a secret the old man had known. His coat pocket had a clip button on the flap, and it had been securely fastened.

He could go mad thinking this through.

The door creaked slightly as he opened it, and he steeled himself for the rush of grief that always awaited him in Toby's room. But today, the emotions were different. He gasped at the strangeness of things, then sat on Toby's bed beside a dozen other broken toys. He looked slowly around the room, and wondered where this new feeling had come from.

He was melancholy rather than sad. Where crushing grief usually compressed his chest and distorted his perception of the surroundings, now there was a cool glow of distance and absence. And for the first time, he could look around the room and see evidence of joy. There on the bookcase was one of his son's drawing books. He'd become adept at sketching, and could draw animals as well as some kids twice his age. *I want to be an artist,* he'd said once, and Ray remembered the pride he'd felt at that moment, as if already acknowledging future achievements. In one corner sat a soccer ball, mud still dried into creases and stitches from the last time they'd kicked it around on the field at the top of the village. Toby had been able to kick the ball almost as far as Ray. They'd laughed as they played, and there were many kids who never had that, whose fathers were too busy or distracted or distant. That was a *good* memory, and though it would not be repeated, Ray felt happy it had happened at all. Toby's life had been short. But he had been loved.

Ray leaned forward and looked at the dusty

carpet between his feet, watching rosettes of tears drop there. But he was smiling, because for the first time in a long while he heard Toby's laughter afresh.

The storm had cleared, blowing itself out during the night, and now the sky was crumbed with the remnants of white clouds. It was still cool, but the weak autumn sun was already drying the paths and streets in random patterns. The harbour was bustling with a bus load of tourists, cameras humming and beeping, faces smiling, heads wearing hats. Ray passed them by and headed into the warren of back streets.

The bakery was on the corner of two narrow streets. It smelled wonderful, and Ray's spirits always lifted a little when he approached. The sun peeked over the buildings behind him and reflected from the upper half of the shop's window, and the lower half was alight with a display of Chelsea buns, cream cakes, custard tarts, fresh crusty rolls, and doughnuts. Part of his reason for coming down was to buy a loaf and a couple of cakes for lunch, but there was another reason. That haunted him, and it seemed to be the only darkness on his mood this morning.

I shouldn't be feeling good, because Toby's dead, he thought. But one thing he and his wife had agreed upon from the beginning—from the start of their new life, not the terrible end of their old one—was that guilt would kill them both. Their son had died of a rare condition no one could have foreseen, and to carry guilt for his death, as well as the grief, would be too much. Acknowledging this had done little to lessen it, however. For the first time today, Ray felt without blame.

"Morning, Rachel," he said, entering the shop.

"Ray! Nice to see you." And then the question that must always come. "How are you?"

"I'm doing okay," he said, smiling. Rachel smiled back. She was an attractive woman, and for years the two of them had conducted what he thought of as distant flirting. But not for some time. He glanced to the rear of the shop where Margaret the owner was unloading loaves from their oven, then back at Rachel. "How're your buns today?" he asked.

"Er . . ." she averted her eyes, and he thought, *Shit, fool, that's just clumsy.* He was the grieving father, the village's figure of unbearable, inconceivable sadness. He had a front to project.

"Soft today, actually," she said quietly.

"Then I'll take four." They exchanged smiles again and he felt better. *Better than ever*, he thought. "How's Ollie? I hear he's been poorly."

Rachel's son Ollie and Toby had gone to school together. They'd been friends. Sometimes Ray would drive them both to school when he knew Rachel had to start work early at the bakery. It had always been a friendship of convenience; Rachel was distant and preoccupied. Not cold, as Elizabeth had suggested, but complex. Ray saw a lot going on in there.

"He's better!" she said. She shook her head, frowning. "One day he's still in bed, and the doctors . . . they're just confused. And then last night he woke up, and that was it. Sat up, wanted ice cream, started complaining when I told him it was bedtime."

"Ha!" Ray said, genuinely pleased for her. "You can tell they're well again when they start protesting."

"Yeah, right," Rachel said, then her gaze flitted away again in discomfort.

"Tell him I say hi," Ray said.

Rachel nodded. Frowned.

"What?" Ray asked.

"He still doesn't quite . . . understand. About Toby."

"None of us do," he said. "But that's okay." He handed her a five pound note, and nodded at the lifeboat collection box when she offered his change. "Rachel . . . you've lived here a long time."

"All my life."

"Is there an old man living up on the moors, above the cliffs?"

"You mean on your side of the village?"

"Yes. Up the coastal path. Only I was up there last night—"

"In the storm?"

"Yeah. I like walking in the dark, it . . . Anyway, I was there and I met an old guy. Really old, like ancient." *And he said things he couldn't have known*, Ray thought, but he did not go that far.

"There's nothing up there that I know of, not close anyway. Once you get on the moors, you can walk back as far as the main road. But the going's tough, and I don't know of any buildings there. Caravan, maybe? Perhaps he's a traveller?"

"Perhaps," Ray said. He took the bag of bread and cakes she handed over the counter, and just for a second their fingers touched. And then the sun welcomed him outside once more.

Need someone to share your cakes with, he thought, but he walked away, and the first sadness of the day descended. Previously, through all the grief of losing his boy, Elizabeth's departure had seemed like just another facet of his new life, not a loss.

He'd seen her yesterday, in the pub with the fisherman. And he had vowed to move on. Today, things had started to feel different.

All because of him, he thought, but the idea was ridiculous. He'd met some mad coot walking in the storm, a weird old sod who was probably losing his marbles. And then the next day when the storm cleared and the sky brightened and he felt good, he attributed it to a midnight, rain-swept meeting. "All in my head," he mumbled, and as a tall, thin woman looked at him, he realized where he was. He'd left the bakery and walked up out of the village, following the single road that curved its way toward the Smuggler's Inn. He hadn't been there since Elizabeth left him, and he'd only driven out of the village a handful of times. He shopped here, lived here, conducted his business from home, and passing his wife's new home always made him feel torn. Now he was walking toward it.

"Huh," Ray said. He stood motionless on the pavement, stream gurgling by on his right. Ducks paddled there, kicking their legs to remain motionless against the flow, and he knew what they felt like. He'd been kicking for a whole year. Maybe now it was time to go with the flow.

When he blinked, the eyes of a broken soldier stared at him. He frowned and blinked again, and a headless Transformer watched from behind his eyes. Moving on meant packing up. Toby's room needed work, and until he'd finished there, he still carried the ghost of his dead son around with him.

And that was the last thing Elizabeth would wish to see.

It took him a while to choose. He thought he'd simply return home and snap up the first toy that came to hand, but he believed that he'd need one with a strong memory attached. The action figures looked too similar—all bulging muscles, camouflage gear, and gripping hands. There was a remote-controlled car with a broken axle, but he couldn't recall Toby ever having played with it. He supposed he must have for the thing to be broken, but maybe he'd played with it on his own. *Or maybe I was so busy I never noticed*, he thought. He chewed on a Chelsea bun, sugar speckling the carpet around his feet as he scanned the room for something suitable.

In the end, he sat on the floor and played with the toys himself. A small plastic warplane did circuits of his head, firing down at the action figures which all slipped for cover beneath the bed. A troop of plastic animals—there'd been a farm building, he was sure, but he had no idea where it was now—stood in line beside his leg, like cattle on parade. A Spider-Man motorcycle that had used to spin and run on its own was propped against the bed leg, Spider-Man nowhere in sight. He hadn't sat and actively played with these toys for ages, and rarely even when Toby was alive. He remembered seeing his son on the living room floor with a riot of colours and shapes splashed across the carpet around him. He'd combine farm animals with Spider-Man, action figures with fluffy toys, and inside his head was a whole world. That world was gone now, and Ray had never been privy to it.

"He died with secrets," he said, and the idea shocked him to the core. He froze, plastic pig in one hand and a yellow metal car in the other, and thought about Toby as an actual person instead of simply his child. He'd been a boy who played and dreamed, loved and imagined, and he had been so utterly wonderful. Ray had always mourned the death of his son as opposed to mourning the death of an individual, as if he'd simply lost something that belonged to him.

The loss of that unique potential was so much worse.

Toby once said he wanted to be a zookeeper when he was older, and there was a broken safari jeep on its roof behind his bedroom door. One door had broken off, long gone, and three of the rubber tires were missing.

"That one," Ray said, vision blurring as he picked up the cold jeep. There was a tiny plastic man behind the wheel, and Toby had said, *One day that will be me, Daddy.*

He didn't even bother with his coat. It was only just past lunchtime, and he had several hours of daylight left. The way was still muddy and slippery. Rain had fallen most of the night, and in steeper places the path showed where water had been flowing like a stream. There were no fresh footprints in this muddy flow, and he felt strangely like an explorer climbing the path for the first time. Behind him lay what he knew—Skentipple, and pain. Ahead . . . who knew what he might find?

It did not seem like the right kind of day to meet that shady old man.

He carried the safari jeep. Slipping a few

times, he let go of it once and it stuck in wet mud. It took him a few minutes to clean it off, using a handkerchief from his pocket and drops of water from a rose bush hanging over a garden wall. When it was clean again, he turned around to look down on the village. There had always been a timelessness to Skentipple that progress could do nothing to take away. A hundred years ago there would have been no cars or modern fishing boats, but the seagulls would have still mobbed the harbour when fishermen came in, and much of the village would have likely looked the same. Some buildings had been reconstructed over time, and added to, but planning restrictions meant that there was rarely anything new being built. It was a village frozen in time, and in such a place perhaps anything was possible.

Maybe he's down there now, wandering the streets and looking for us, Ray thought. The idea of his son lost and frightened was awful, and he didn't know where it had come from. He turned and walked on, climbing harder until he was panting, concentrating on every step to avoid slipping again.

The path levelled out and became muddier. He took each step gently, arms held out to either side for balance, and so he only saw the man when he almost walked into him.

"Bit nicer this afternoon," the old man said.

Ray stared at him, unable to reply. He was dressed in old jeans and a thick woollen jumper, boots that reached to his knees, and a scarf wrapped casually around his neck. A flat cap sat perched on his head, more for affectation than warmth. Sparse hairs sprouted from beneath it, and in daylight he looked even older than he had in the dark.

"I . . ." Ray said. "I didn't think I'd see you."

"Still brought that, though," the man said, nodding at the safari jeep.

Ray looked at the toy in his hand, then away again. He hid it down by his side, behind his leg, like an alcoholic caught with a bag-wrapped bottle.

"Thank you for returning the Ben 10

watch," Ray said. His voice was firm, definite, offering no chance for the man to deny it.

"A pleasure," he said. "Took me all night. Wasn't just the missing spring and its broken mounting. Turns out . . ." He waved at the air, as if searching for a word. "Circuit board thing was fried, and the LED was smashed from where the boy sat on it that time."

"What?" Ray asked. *The boy? Sat on it? What did he mean?*

"Oh," the old man said through an embarrassed smile. "Maybe he didn't tell you."

Ray wanted to rant and rage. He wanted to shout at the old man, grasp handfuls of his woollen jumper and swing him against the low stone wall bounding the path, where he would scream and beat the truth out of him. But something about that smile gave Ray pause, and he thought perhaps it was he who would end up being held against the wall.

"*Why* did you fix it?"

"To help you keep your promise to your son."

"How can you know I promised to mend it?"

The man's eyes grew a little darker, as if living an uncomfortable memory. "Because every parent promises that when a child breaks a toy."

It's all hidden away, Ray thought. *He's talking, but saying nothing.* "So . . . how old are you?" he asked instead. He wasn't sure where the question had come from, but he found himself examining the man's wrinkles and sparse hair, distracting himself from difficult questions.

"Older than I look," the man said. His face fell a little, and he glanced over Ray's shoulders at the village behind him.

"I'll walk back down with you," Ray said.

"No, no need. I wasn't visiting the village just now. Just come down to meet you."

"You brought the watch back to me last night?"

The man smiled, nodded, shrugged, a master of mixed messages. *And if I give him the safari jeep?* Ray thought. *Do I really want to?*

"What do you know of my son?" he asked instead.

"That you miss him," the old man said, and true sadness sculpted his face into something different. He looked down at the village again. "That your life has been different since he went. That your sadness marks you, just as surely as happiness or illness or the knowledge of violence marks other people. I know that the best way to reach people is through their imagination, and the most solid home of imagination is a child's toys. And what I do has helped."

Ray scoffed, but he thought of how he'd felt this morning in Toby's bedroom, and down in the village, and how he'd found himself walking toward Elizabeth. To see her? To offer a hand of peace? He wasn't sure, because he'd turned around and come back home.

And what harm could it do? Really, what harm?

"I'm walking," he said, nodding past the old man and along the cliff path. "Join me?"

"With pleasure," the man said.

Ray started ahead, walking hard. The old man kept pace with him, and Ray thought, *If I walk fast he'll wear out, and when he's weak and sitting by the path I can question him more.* But as the damp path slipped and squelched beneath their boots, and Ray felt his body growing hot beneath the layers, the old man hardly seemed to break a sweat. He followed on behind, and now and then Ray heard small gasps that might have been laughs. He did not turn around to see. He knew where he was going, though not why, and he was determined to reach there soon.

"What's your name?" he asked.

"Don't have much use for one."

"That doesn't mean you don't *have* one," Ray said, covering his surprise.

The old man was silent for a while, the thump of their footsteps the only sound. Above them a seagull called. Out at sea a speedboat thumped from wave to wave.

"So?" Ray asked.

"Hold up," the man said, and Ray smiled to himself. *Tired him out*, he thought. But when he turned around, he saw that was not the case at all. The old man stood staring at him, one foot propped on a raised stone in the path, hat cocked at a jaunty angle, and a look behind his smile that said, *I know exactly what you were trying to do.*

"Not far now," the old man said. "Up past that rise, then the hut's down close to the cliff's edge."

"Hut?"

"The place you think I might . . . use."

He was right. Ray had that place in mind, the overgrown stone structure he'd seen nine months ago when he'd made his way down toward the cliffs and death. Something about it had worried at him last night, a dream he could not recall that left dregs of itself imprinted, suggestions for the day by a voice he could not hear. And he had thought maybe the old man lived there, a relatively smart tramp. He looked him up and down, and though the clothes weren't new or even expensive, they were certainly clean. The old guy took notice of his appearance.

"So what *is* your name?"

"Well," the man said, flicking the hat back on his head and scratching his scalp, "I'll bet you've not had so much need for yours lately. Have you?"

No, Ray thought. *Elizabeth not there, I've closed myself off, and today* . . . Down at the bakery, Rachel, that was the first time he recalled someone using his name for days, perhaps weeks.

"So my name is as important to me now as . . . where I was born. The shoes I wore three years ago. The dream I had a year ago last Christmas." The old man shrugged, and in that dismissive gesture Ray saw a level of complete control, and calm confidence.

The safari jeep had grown warm in his hand, absorbing heat through his skin, and something made him look down at it. The last time it had been this warm was when Toby was playing with it, and a rush of emotions shuddered through him. *That'll be me one day, Daddy*, he'd said, squinting through the scratched plastic window at the featureless man cast behind the steering wheel.

"You know I can help it," the man said. He held out his hand. "There's no need for you to . . ." He nodded sideways, toward the cliff edge and the mounds of undergrowth there, hiding whatever it hid. "Not yet, at least. Maybe next time, when you're more settled, and you need to see so you can take it on. Maybe then."

"Take it on?"

The old man looked tired, at last, and something else. Unsettled. Even nervous. "The toy?"

For a moment, Ray thought of throwing the toy jeep toward the cliffs and then running back the way they'd come. But he was scared that he'd arrive home and find it on his doorstop, broken door fixed, three bare tires rounded with rubber once more. So he placed it gently in the old man's hand and mourned the loss of warm metal against his skin.

"Hmm," the old man said in satisfaction. He nodded to Ray, then looked past him along the path. *Time for you to leave*, that look said. Ray wanted to defy him, to stay here and watch while he did whatever it was he did up here. But that would defeat the object. He'd brought the jeep here for this reason, and now it was time to go.

"Whatever it is you do . . ." he said, and the nameless man raised an eyebrow, a faint smile on his lips. *He's laughing at me*, Ray thought.

"What?" the man said.

"It works," Ray said. And he turned and marched back along the path, heading for the village and the safe comfort of his house. With every step he took, something drew him back, a desire to understand, to witness. It wasn't long before he stopped and turned around.

The man stood where he'd left him, in exactly the same position. He waved Ray on. Ray, feeling like a schoolchild, continued on his way, but stopped again after twenty paces.

This time, the man was gone.

His hand suddenly very cold, as if it had never held that jeep at all, Ray ran back up the slippery path. He reached the place where he and the old man had stood and there was no sign that he had ever been there—no boot prints in the mud, no scent of old clothes on the air. He stood on tiptoes to look toward the cliff edge, trying to make out the mound of undergrowth that marked the location of the old stone building. There was something . . . an intimation of regularity, though he could not quite see the stone itself. He tried pushing through the undergrowth—gorse, bracken, ferns fading away to winter—but they snagged at his clothing and pricked his skin. There was no clear path through, and the old man could never have forced his way past this quickly.

Ray looked up the cliff path, and it was empty as far as he could see. He supposed the old man might have run and reached the place where it turned out of sight. He might have.

But he'd have had to run very quickly.

He pushed some more, stretching, tugging branches and clumps of gorse aside and pricking his fingers in the process. A dozen blood droplets formed on his hands, smearing as he tried to haul himself close to the cliff's edge. But he was held back, and eventually he retreated to the path. He was panting from exertion, heart racing from something more.

"Damn it," Ray said, looking around for the man, seeing the place where that old stone hut just might be. Then he turned and walked slowly back down to the village.

Later, as he sat waiting on his doorstep, he watched the old woman climbing up from the village. She smiled wearily, made no comment about his nakedness that morning, mentioned only the weather and the cold. And he watched her go, wondering what dreams would come.

4

After an unsettled evening trying to read, trying to watch TV, trying to concentrate on anything, but finding his attention drawn again and again out into the falling darkness, Ray went at last to bed.

When he woke up the next day he stretched, unwilling to relinquish the comforting warmth beneath the duvet for the chill bedroom air. He'd woken with an erection and a dissolving dream involving Rachel from the bakery, and he smiled at the brightening room, sighing contentedly. He supposed he'd always had a crush on her, like an excitable teen instead of the forty-something he was. He had no memory of the dream, just a feeling, and it shrank away in the promise of a new day.

At last he stood up from his bed, shrugging on a dressing gown and padding to the toilet. After urinating he walked back to his room, enjoying the feel of the landing floorboards on his bare feet. Wood was never cold, just cool, whatever the temperature outside. He had always liked being this close to things. Carpets were fine, but walking on them barefoot he always felt as though he were separated from the body of the house. The wood was its skeleton, carpet merely clothing.

Dressing, Ray frowned at a memory hovering just beyond his perception. He paused with one leg in, one leg out of his jeans. *What was that?* Something forced itself toward him, a memory he should clasp, and he blinked in surprise at the suddenness of the vision that struck him: Rachel from the bakery slipping off her blouse with flour-covered hands, her smile promising more. *That's not it*, he thought, frowning the dream-memory away. *There's something else, it wasn't that, it was never that.*

It was halfway down the stairs, as he saw the yellow toy safari jeep sitting on the fourth step up from the bottom, that he remembered he'd once had a son.

And Toby was like a dream fading in instead of out. There was a boy without a face or voice, and he had gone somewhere. Then his face emerged in Ray's memory, freckled in the summer, blond hair made lighter by the sun, and he shouted in glee as he tipped bucket after bucket of water onto the flower bed, mud pies much more interesting to him than daffodil bulbs.

"Toby," Ray breathed as he sat down on the stairs. He bent forward slowly and picked up the jeep, wondering how the hell he could have woken up and not remembered his dead son. Every morning since Toby had died, Ray had surfaced with the boy's laughter or tears on his mind, and the knowledge of his death pressing him down like the greatest weight. Some mornings he had risen from sleep that had itself been infected with that dreadful knowledge, and sometimes—the meanest of times—he had dreamed that Toby was alive and well and laughing, and the waking had been unbearable.

But this morning he had come awake like a contented man.

"Tobes," he said, "I do love you so much." He cried, but they were not bitter tears, nor even tears driven by anger at himself. They stopped quickly and he went to the kitchen, nursing the mended toy as the kettle boiled. A new door had been fixed on, and the three new tires exactly matched the one remaining— shapes, make, treads. He turned the jeep this way and that, trying to see any mark or clue the old man might have left as to how he'd done it. But there was nothing.

He was in my house, Ray thought. *He was here, inside, while I slept.* But that did not frighten or concern him as much as it should have. While the tea was brewing he went upstairs to his dead son's room. Broken toys were still scattered across the bed and floor where Ray had left them the previous day, and he smiled sadly as he sat on the bed, picking them up at random, remembering. Here was the Power Ranger whose arm had come off when Elizabeth stepped on it, Toby's cry of grief heartbreaking to both of them. They'd comforted him, given him a chocolate bar, and Ray had promised to fix it, but never had. Here was the self-propelling car whose mechanism had become jammed, and Toby had cried because it no longer moved on its own. *It's dead*, he'd said, and Ray had not fixed that one, either.

On the side of the wardrobe, which still held many of Toby's little clothes, was a self-portrait he'd painted in school when he was five years old. It was the usual childish splodge of paint; big round pink head, bright blue eyes, smiling mouth with—much to Ray's and Elizabeth's amusement at the time—two long vampirish teeth. Since he'd gone, Ray had not been able to look at it without crying. It was something more than a photograph, evidence of Toby's mind working, his hands moving, and a sign of the self-awareness he'd barely had time to explore. But now he looked at it and smiled, and his dead son smiled back. At least he'd had a chance. At least he'd spent some years on this planet, instead of no years at all. He'd known laughter and joy, and he had been loved.

Ray gathered some toys to him and rested back on the bed, looking around the room with new eyes and finding in himself an ability to celebrate—instead of only mourn—Toby's life.

"Elizabeth," he said. Something about his estranged wife's name had changed. It held more meaning than it did yesterday, when it had simply been the first name of the woman who'd left him. Today it was Toby's mother, part of this room, these toys, and part of Toby's mind when he'd picked up the fat paintbrush and painted himself as he believed his mother and father saw him. "Elizabeth," Ray said again. And he knew he had to talk to her.

His walk through the village was alive with memories, and Ray wondered whether in his grief he'd been burying them so deep that they were as good as forgotten. They came to the fore now, bright sunlit moments of pushing Toby's pram, guiding him on unsteady, unlearned legs, and chasing after him when he progressed from toddler to little boy. The most obscure, meaningless recollections hit home, and Ray realized that no moment is meaningless. His son's smile over his shoulder as he entered the local post office holding his mother's hand, skipping along the curbside with one foot on pavement and one on road, kneeling down with bread in his hand and a robin hopping cautiously closer, closer . . . each of these images was precious, because they were evidence of his son's life. Toby was gone now, but memories could be as rich and as meaningful as experience. After all, every instant that passed—every step Ray took, every beat of his heart—was instantly consigned to memory.

He passed the bakery and paused to look inside, but he could not see Rachel. Perhaps on the way back he'd call in to see her, after he'd spoken with Elizabeth and . . .

"What am I going to say?" he whispered, walking on past the bakery and staring at the ground before him. He couldn't tell the truth. That he'd met an old man on the cliffs, and that the old man was fixing Toby's toys and somehow easing Ray's grief. That was ridiculous. The very idea lessened their loss, but much as Ray dwelled on the reality of what was happening as he walked, he could not change the way he felt. Something was lifting from him.

He worked his way through the winding streets and onto the road that curved out of the village. He'd decide what to say when he got there. Planning these things would never work, and he'd have to trust himself. They had such a history, so much love between them, and he'd always thought of their relationship as something that had paused rather than ended. There had *been* no ending; no shouting, arguing, or severing of ties. Elizabeth had simply moved out and on, but perhaps their past was not yet beyond reach.

"We could have another," Ray whispered, and his breath caught in his throat. He stood frozen by the roadside, trying to imagine Toby with a brother or sister. The idea was a shocking acknowledgement of there being a future.

The day moved on, and when he reached the Smugglers' Inn, he sat on a bench in the small beer garden, feeling damp soaking through his trousers, staring at the façade, wondering where Elizabeth was now and which room was hers. It was approaching midday, and a family of tourists was perusing the menu board, father silent, mother distracted, two kids laughing and joking. Ray thought of the old smuggling tunnel the landlord Tony Fox had shown him an age ago, and wondered why he never made more use of it with the tourists. Maybe some things were too private.

The pub door opened and Elizabeth emerged. Ray caught his breath. She carried several ashtrays and started laying them on the tables, and she actually passed him by before pausing, turning back, and realizing who he was.

"Ray," she said, and her eyes filled up. *I remind her of him*, he thought. "What are you . . . ?"

"I came to see you," he said.

"Why?" She could not quite look at him; her eyes flickered from side to side, as if in the sudden presence of her estranged husband she sought her son's ghost.

"Because . . . there's life beyond. We don't have to let it beat us. Destroy us. Toby wouldn't have wanted—"

"Don't say his name," she breathed, staring right at him for the first time.

"Toby?"

"Don't." A plea.

"Don't be afraid of his memory, Liz." He stood and walked toward her, hands coming up to hold her arms. She backed away.

"I can't . . . I can't even . . ." She shook

her head, and Ray thought she was going to crumple. He prepared to catch her, ease her onto a bench where they could sit and talk. But then she started shouting. "Just leave me alone! You have no idea! You just don't know. How can you even . . . *smile*?"

Was I smiling? Ray thought, but he frowned and backed away. Elizabeth was not crying. Her face was red, and her hands worked by her side, clawing.

"It's something we have to come to terms with," he said. "Smiling isn't forgetting him. We can move on, without dishonouring his memory. He was our little boy, Liz, and the last thing he'd want—"

"He's dead!" she shouted, as if believing he'd forgotten all they'd gone through.

There's a man up on the cliffs, he thought, but there was no way he could say that, not even now.

"Can't we just talk?" he asked.

"You know we can't," she said. She glanced sidelong at the parents who'd been perusing the menu board. They were leading their children away, trying to distract their fascinated kids from the shouting woman. "I just can't, not with you. You remind me of him so much."

"That's a bad thing?" he asked.

"Yeah." He thought she'd shout her reply, scream it, but it was little more than a gasp.

"And Jason?"

Elizabeth stared at him then, and it was the first time she'd looked at him like that since leaving. She wore the old Elizabeth behind her expression, not the grief-stricken shell she had become, and for a second he allowed himself hope.

And then she shot it down.

"Jason helps me forget." She turned and went back into the pub, shutting him out. He sat down, clasped his hands on the wet bench, and stared down at them for a long time.

From above, we follow him down below. He walks along the road like something defeated, but as he nears the harbour his shoulders straighten, his head lifts, and perhaps there's a smile on his lips. He walks faster. He smells dead things, because that's much of what the sea's smell is—a familiar and nostalgic scent. He wonders whether the sea has always smelled the same, even before humans settled here hundreds, thousands of years ago. *Almost*, he guesses. Though without humans here to sense, did the sea even smell at all?

He starts climbing the path that leads up onto the hillside, where his home is balanced amongst many others, walls set into precarious footings, the buildings huddled and clinging like eager observers of the harbour down below. Up beyond his home, the path to the cliffs is empty for now. There are footprints in the mud, and a seagull is cracking a shelled thing against a rock tucked beneath a gorse bush at the path's edge. Its own feet add more delicate prints as it dances back and forth, picking up the sea creature in its beak, dropping it on the rock, again and again. It knows that it could take flight and drop it from a greater height, but already the slick saltiness of the shell's innards is exposed and leaking. A few more impacts and it will be able to prise the thing apart and swallow the insides.

The sounds reach the old man's ears where he stands up on the cliff path looking out to sea. We know that he is waiting for someone who will come from a different direction. The old man has intrigued, has entwined the younger man's perception like a blade of grass around his finger, and now it is time to finish.

He sighs and waits, and hopes that this time it will work. He has been doing these things for far too long.

This time he took a brightly coloured toy that was supposed to be a hand-held saw. When it was pushed across the floor, the wheel beneath would turn, lights would flash, and it made a saw-like buzzing. Ray had bought it for his son on a work trip to the States, and it had been well-used over the following few months. Then one day, it had stopped working. He'd changed the batteries, to no avail. He took the thing apart, but he'd never been that handy, and the electronics of the thing just confused him. He saw no loose wires or broken connections, and he remembered screwing the toy back together thinking, *It'll work now; I've taken it apart, put it back together, and it'll work, and I'll never know what was wrong.* But it had not worked, and after an evening sulking about it, he thought perhaps Toby had never considered it again.

He slammed the front door behind him, didn't bother locking it, strode up the hillside. Ray had never been as fit as he would have liked, and by the time the path levelled out, he was sweating and panting, but eager to reach his goal.

It was mid-afternoon. The old man was waiting for him, dressed in jeans and a shirt, a light coat, and walking boots. He smiled gently as Ray approached, then held out his hand.

"Here," Ray said. "Whatever it is you do . . ." He placed the colourful plastic toy in the man's hand, and stepped back.

The old man looked down at the saw for a few seconds, and his face was so expressionless that Ray's guts sank, his shoulders slumped, and he thought, *Has anything been happening here at all?* The man turned the toy this way and that, and sunlight shone between clouds and glinted from its garish colours.

"Come with me," he said at last. He lifted the toy, then nodded out toward the sea. "Something to show you."

"Come with you where?"

But today, the old man was not wasting words. He turned and walked farther along the cliff, and then turned right from the path and forced his way into the plants growing thick at its edge. They seemed hardly to touch him, and when he glanced back to see if Ray was following, there was a strange look in his eyes. He appeared almost nervous.

"Not far," he said. "You've seen it before.

Not been there, but seen it. And now I've something to show you."

Ray glanced at the gorse, the hawthorn bushes.

"It's easy if you know where to tread," the old man said.

So Ray followed, because he had the sense that this was the culmination of something, or the beginning of something new. At first he tried to judge just where the old man was stepping and follow his lead, but he soon found that the plants appeared to be parting around his legs. There was no sense of movement, no sound of them rustling or twisting out of his way, but his route was unimpeded. He stared at the old man's back and, past him, the sea. Moments later, he saw the angular shoulder of the stone hut.

"Home, sweet home," the man said, chuckling. There was something not quite right about that sound, and Ray paused, the plants suddenly pressing in around him again. A thorn stuck into his thigh; a stem was curled around his ankle. As he tried to pull back, he was pricked and spiked again, more wounds to add to the scabbed punctures on his fingers and hands.

"Come on, now," the old man said. "You want to know what it is I do, don't you?"

Ray looked from him to the overgrown structure, and back again.

"Don't you?"

Ray nodded. He moved forward, and the man let him.

"Then step inside," he said. "Gotta fix this broken toy."

He waited until Ray stood beside him. They were maybe ten feet from the cliff here, the actual edge blurred by the plants that grew out over the terrible drop. *I thought about stepping from there once*, he thought, and looked back along the cliff to where he'd stood.

"Two men built it almost seventy years ago," the old man said. "They were already middle-aged then. Fishermen, they'd seen the cruelties man can inflict on man in the mud of Ypres. So when the second war started, they wanted to do their part. Fish, they were told, help to feed our nation. But fishing to them was like breathing to us. It seemed . . . helpless. So they built this thing as well, and for the duration of the war, they took turns sitting up here, watching." He looked out to sea at the three large ships on the horizon, and the smaller vessels bobbing closer in.

"How do you know all that?" Ray asked.

"Because I came here, and sat here, and they told me." He stared at Ray as if challenging him to question.

"So why bring me here now?"

The old man looked again at the broken toy in his hand, and this time he seemed to give it serious attention. He turned it this way and that, held it up to the light, shook it, breathed onto it, and then held still, as if listening.

"To show you how this whole thing works," the old man said. "To show you how to perform wonders." He edged past the hawthorn tree crowding the end of the stone building, and

Ray followed.

He didn't know what to expect when they walked inside; he'd spent no time contemplating it. The instant before he saw, he imagined the insides to be overtaken with nature. There was no roof to the shelter—whatever had been built there had long-since collapsed and been subsumed—and the heads of the walls were crumbled by frost and plant growth. Inside might lie the rotting remains of the roof, piled into the corners and smothered with plants. Perhaps some wild rose bushes might have taken hold, sheltering against the walls. It was possible that the place had been found and used by lovers or drinkers, or those who simply wanted to be alone, and maybe evidence of their loving or solitude was still there—initials carved into the walls, an atmosphere of melancholy.

What he saw was so far removed from what he had, briefly, imagined that he paused and closed his eyes, waiting for the image to vanish. But when he looked again, he saw the same view, and he had to concede that this was the truth.

The inside of the ruined stone building had been completely cleared out. There was a table at its centre, as tall as a dining room table though much smaller, and a chair tucked beneath it. Something sat on the table shrouded with a soft chamois leather. Beside it, fixed to the end wall, was a large glass-fronted cabinet containing an array of tools. Such was his shock that Ray could not accurately make out shape or purpose; he simply saw the glint of metal and the shine of well-used wooden handles. There were other things in there too, made of material he wasn't quite so sure of. But his attention was quickly snatched from the strange cabinet by the other, stranger display that took up the back wall.

Hung from hooks on a fine metal mesh were dozens of toys. There were dolls and teddies, action figures and ballerinas, cars and models, and others Ray could not identify. They took his breath away. Each of them seemed to be broken, with limbs missing or plastic cracked, and they formed an orderly queue awaiting the man who would fix them.

The old man stood quietly by his side.

"How long have you . . . ?" Ray asked.

"I've been here a while. Not too long, though. I move around."

"And all these . . . all from Skentipple?"

"Some," the man said. "Some are from the surrounding area, or from places a long time ago. There are always toys that can't be fixed."

Ray's eyes were drawn again and again to the chamois-covered object on the table. It was a mystery he wanted to uncover, but it was also something safe to look at. The toys and the tools, they were unreal, and—

Impossible? he thought. *Really? And why is that?*

The old man walked forward, his feet scratching grit across the smooth timber floor. He pulled out the chair and sat down. He seemed instantly at ease, comfortable where he was, as much a part of the tableau as everything else. With the old man in the picture, everything Ray saw started to make sense.

The man moved the chamois aside, and on the table lay the broken toy saw.

"But you just carried that in here!" Ray said. He looked on the ground around him, looking to see where the old man had dropped the real saw. Then he darted forward and snatched it up from the table. Turning it this way and that, depressing the button on the broken object, he saw a scrape here, a dent there, and he recognized them both.

"Let me," the old man said, taking it gently from his hands.

"But what about all these?" Ray asked, nodding at the back wall. "Aren't they all first?"

"I get to decide what deserves my attention first," he said. "I . . . prioritize. Doing so is freedom, but it's also sometimes part of my curse. So watch. Learn. I brought you here because you need to take over when I'm gone."

"What?"

"Such wonders, here," he said. "I know you'll welcome them."

"But—"

"Watch," the old man said quieter. "Learn." And he went about fixing the toy.

A million questions crowded in, confusing Ray, making him queasy and dizzy. But the moment the man opened the tool cabinet by his side, Ray was enrapt. He watched in wonder, questions and concerns ushered back and hidden away for a while in the darker corners of his mind.

Some of the tools were obvious, but the man quickly started using things—*doing* things—that made no sense. Ray frowned, squinting, trying to see past the strange actions and understand the weird implements. But moments later, the man sat back and the toy was alone on the table before him, and Ray was none the wiser.

"That's it?" he asked.

"You weren't watching?" The old man

turned the toy on and pushed it gently across the table. A buzz-saw noise rose and fell, lights flashed through its speckled plastic case. Ray closed his eyes, because the last time he'd heard that, Toby had been alive. When he looked again, only a second or two later, the man stood before him, holding out the toy in his hand.

"Here," he said. "For you." He looked very tired. He hadn't before—until now, Ray had marvelled at how good the old man looked— but he suddenly seemed faded. His skin was paler, his eyes deeper. "And now I've done for you, I want you to do for me."

"Do what?" Ray asked.

"Take over. I'm old, and . . ." The man looked back at the toys still hanging on the wall. "And I can't help everyone. It's not fair. It was never part of the deal."

"Deal?"

"Say you will," the man said, intense. "Say you will, and I'll tell you everything. How it came about, the grief that consumed me, the

joy I felt when he came and asked me to . . ."
He waved at the toys, gaze never once leaving
Ray's eyes.

"I can't," Ray said, not a refusal, simply a
statement of fact.

"You *must!*" the man said. He came close,
and for the first time Ray was scared of
him. He was old, yes, and he looked like the
next sea breeze would break him. But there
was something about him—there always
had been—that seemed not quite here. Not
quite right. A distance in his eyes, perhaps,
but a power in his stance as well. He might
have weaker, older muscles, but there was a
strength to him that defied understanding.
And now he scared Ray to death.

Ray backed away three or four steps,
feet leaving the wooden floor boarding and
tangling in plants and roots. The old man
stopped and grinned, something twinkling in
his eyes. And Ray felt the weight of nothing
behind him.

He glanced back quickly and dizziness hit

him. *Three more steps and I'd have been over,* he thought, and the sea surged into the cliffs two hundred feet below him. Months back, that would have been his wish, but now he suddenly had something to live for. He wasn't sure what, but he did understand that this old man had given it to him.

"Really," Ray said, hands out in a pleading gesture. "Thank you. *Thank* you! But . . ." He nodded at the strange open room, the tools, the broken toys. "I just can't. I don't know any of this."

"You think I did when it happened to me?" the man said. He didn't shout, and Ray thought he probably never had. He conveyed the world in a whisper. "I'm *trapped* here," he said, and he seemed suddenly hopeless, wretched. A thing of power in bondage.

"I'm sorry," Ray said. He started away from the stone hut, along the cliff parallel to the edge. It was tough going, and he kept glancing back at the man watching him from the tumbled front façade of the strange

building. *How did he get those things in there?*
Ray thought. *How does he keep them dry, keep it
safe? How does he* live *in there?* But losing sight
of the tool cabinet and the incongruous timber
flooring seemed to erase them from his mind.

"I can take it all back," the man said. "Don't
think because I've fixed your memories they're
yours forever."

"You didn't fix my *memories!*" Ray said.

"Think what you like. Just . . . won't you
listen? Can't you just *hear* me?" He was not
quite pleading. Not quite.

Ray was thigh-high in undergrowth.
Thorns pricked at him, and looking down
he couldn't understand how he'd become so
entangled.

"Please?" the old man said.

Ray pushed on toward home, and the
safety of precious memories. Never for an
instant would he consider what the old man
had asked. Never for a moment could it be a
possibility. And when he looked up again, the
old man was gone.

"Hello?" Ray shouted. There was no answer. "Hey. You still there?" But there were no sounds here other than the cliff sounds, the sea sounds, and the breath of the breeze. He stared at the stone building, trying to discern anything out of the ordinary. Could the walls he looked at really be lined with broken toys on the other aside? He thought not. Were there really plants ripped from the mortar, timber flooring laid, furniture installed? Of course not. That was ridiculous, product of some part of his mind he'd lost sight of since Toby's death. That part was making itself known again, dragging him from the brink of despair in a subconscious attempt to rescue his own sanity.

It was all in his head.

"And now I'm stuck out here," he said. Laughter rumbled inside. He swallowed it, but it was persistent. He noticed a flash of colour closer to the cliff path, just a few feet away, and as he worked his way toward it—ignoring the pain, and ignoring that fact that he'd been hallucinating something so clear, so defined— he realized what it was. The saw toy.

He plucked the toy from the bushes and placed his thumb on the switch. He paused only for a moment, and then flicked it on. Broken. Of course.

How could he think anything else?

It was late afternoon by the time he arrived home. Not sure exactly where all the time had gone, Ray locked the door and dropped the toy saw into the kitchen bin. He'd have no need of it again, and neither would Toby. Keeping things like that just for the sake of it was foolish. Backward-thinking.

"There's no way I could have done it," he said to the silent house, when what he'd meant to say was, *There's no way that could have happened.*

He switched the kettle on and went up to the bathroom, ran a bath, dumped a load of bath salts in, and thought of the bottle of merlot sitting in the pantry. A long warm bath, a couple of glasses of wine . . .

He paused in the bathroom doorway and thought of Toby. A sadness filled him, but a quiet sadness. *I wish you were here, little lad*, he thought. *I so wish you'd never died and the three of us were all here together, as was meant to be.* But he was alone in the house. Maybe it wouldn't always be that way, but for now it was what he had.

"Some music," he said, because he did not like the silence.

Music playing, wine bottle opened and set on the closed toilet seat with a large glass, Ray lowered himself into the scalding bath with a sigh. He intended to dwell upon what had or had not happened, to analyze, and to consider where and when things had started to change.

Instead, he slept. And in his dreams, he heard the sounds of Toby playing with his toys in his bedroom, the electrical beeps and whistles and growls, and just as the dream went bad, he heard Toby's delighted laughter for the very last time.

5

We see that it's another stormy night in Skentipple, and its residents are battening down the hatches. In her room upstairs in the Smugglers' Inn, Elizabeth is performing vigorous fellatio on Jason, who sits on the edge of the bed gasping in delight. He was only in the room for a few seconds before she reached for him, and he's glad, partly because he's getting a blowjob and *any* guy is glad for that, and partly because Elizabeth seems to have emerged from that reflective state she's been in for a while. She can't help it, he knows, because what happened to her and Ray was terrible, but sometimes he wonders if he did the right thing getting mixed up with her afterward. It was friendship at first, and then the momentum of desire caught them. He wonders what has happened today that changed the way she was, but he doesn't question it too much. He looks down at her bobbing head and bare shoulder, bathed in flashes of moonlight between fast-drifting clouds.

We move up and away from the frantic lovers, out through the window, and the wind snags us. We go with the flow and let it pull us quickly down toward the sea. That's unusual— the breeze usually comes *from* the sea—and sometimes when its direction shifts, it means something unpleasant is about to happen. That's an old wives' tale, but fishermen live, work, and breathe for their old wives.

The road below is glistening with first rainfall, and the clouds rolling above promise plenty more. We see vague shapes moving below, seeking the unique shelter of home. They all have stories to tell, most of them amazing, but none of them concerns us tonight. They tell their tales to the darkness. Skentipple will lose its power soon, a regular occurrence during storms, and a thousand candles will burn away a little more of their lives until it comes back on.

We arrive above the house clasped to the hillside just as the door bursts open. The man stands there in the doorway, disbelief twisting his features, and anger, and an impression that something is drawing to a close. His hands are fisted at his side, and he seems to be examining his garden, searching for something, scanning the deepening darkness for something that isn't there.

While he was in the bath, something was taken.

We drift down closer to see what, and by whom, all the while knowing that some stories are by necessity left unfinished, and that some have their endings taken away by force. It's a sad time. Something is indeed drawing to a close. And if only he knew, Ray would be grasping every frame of memory as if his life depended on it.

"Bastard!" Ray shouted. *"Bastard!"* He ran uphill, leaving Skentipple behind again, feet slipping on the rain-slicked path. *He came into my house while I was* in the bath!

The water had been cool when he awoke, bubbles popped away to nothing, wine glass barely touched. The house had felt different. He hadn't been able to pin down just how it had changed, but he had dried and dressed quickly, and then wandered into Toby's room.

Every broken toy was gone. Every broken part was gone too; the springs and snapped plastic, wheels and arms, those bits that had been retained with the toys so they could be fixed one day. There was a sheen of fluff and dust on the floor beside the bed, and the duvet was crumpled and dusty where he'd laid out a selection of the toys. The plastic box from beneath the bed was still there, empty.

And Ray knew who had taken them. If he could come here at night and leave a mended toy, surely he could enter and steal them all away.

So he ran to find the old man, because whatever he had done—with the Ben 10 watch, the safari jeep, and the plastic saw toy—he was now little more than a thief.

The rain cooled him, but did not touch Ray's anger. What did the bastard expect of him? How could he possibly think that he could take over whatever strange thing the old fucker even *did*? It seemed all so unreasonable, and Ray had not even asked for any help.

Yet he *had* been helped, and there was no denying that. Ray had no clue how any of it had worked. Perhaps it was simply a subtle psychological nudge: get him to remember his promise to his dead son—*I'll fix your toy tomorrow, Buddy*—and from there a gradual acceptance, a gentle moving on. But he thought not. He thought there was something much more to whatever it was the old man had done, and it was the stuff of storms and wind and deepening shadows, not sunlight and cheerful remembrance.

He left the village behind and slowed, following the path in the fading light. This was what the old man wanted, he knew, but his anger drew him on. Fear nestled inside, but Ray shoved it away. The bastard had come into his house . . . touched Toby's toys . . . taken them, without invite or offer. And if he'd done so to cause a confrontation, then the fucker would get just that.

Ray reopened scabbed wounds as he forced himself through the bushes and hawthorns, shoving toward the cliff's edge and not caring how close he might be, hearing the rain pattering close, and the rumble of waves eroding the land far away, and down. The stone structure stood there, a shadow against the sea, and from this angle, there was no sign of light. *How can there be? He can't be there, just sitting, just welcoming the storm.*

Ray forged forward. The light was fading fast, and the rain was heavier than ever, but seeing the building, he was better able to locate the cliff edge. Water ran into his eyes and he blinked it away. His legs hurt, his ankles and feet grabbed by a hundred roots, but eventually he reached the back of the stone building and climbed. He found a foothold and reached up, hands pressing down atop the wall. Pushing, pulling, he rose.

There was nothing there. The building's exposed interior was completely overgrown. He climbed higher so he could lean across the head of the wall, picturing it crumbling and collapsing and trapping him here in the storm. But the wall held, allowing him to look down and see only plants growing from it, not metal racking and hooks and toys.

"Damn it!" Ray shouted, but there was no one, and nothing there to hear. Rain ran down the back of his neck and plastered his hair to his head. He was struck by a sudden, overwhelming sense of hopelessness—the old man had gone, and now any chance at control had been ripped away. By coming here and confronting him, perhaps Ray might have been able to exert some influence over things. But the old man was gone, leaving Ray alone, and the unfairness of it all made him shout.

The storm swallowed his voice. After

a while, he left that old tumbled-down building—a place he could not imagine having been occupied for decades—and made his way back down to Skentipple. On that twenty-minute walk in torrential rain and an occasional flash of lightning from far out at sea, the possibility of madness presented itself to him yet again. His mind was playing with him, conjuring a complex escape from crippling grief, building layer upon layer of make-believe and somehow losing itself in the process. They would see him arriving back at the village, watching from warm rooms hidden behind twitching curtains as that poor man walked down, sodden from the cliffs, and they'd whisper that one day he'd go up there and they'd never see him again, the implication an echo of a time he'd believed that himself.

But though certainties hovered around him and never quite settled, like dancing raindrops, he held on to the knowledge of what he would find at home—the mended toys. He would hold them and know the truth, and Toby would smile in his dreams and welcome his father back.

Rain flowed down the path like a new stream, carrying him back to his house. Inside, it was dark and lonely. He turned on every light, stripped off his soaked clothes, slung a heavy dressing gown around his shoulders and built a fire in the hearth.

The fixed toys would be on the cabinet beside Toby's bed. He would grab them soon, return downstairs, and curl on the sofa with the bottle of wine from earlier, listening to Toby's laughter in the rain. *I like the wet*, his son had said once, splashing and giggling.

"I like the wet too," Ray said, but as he finally pushed open Toby's bedroom door and saw the empty space where the toys had been, he forgot where those words had come from.

Ray awoke the next morning in an unfamiliar bed, with unfamiliar scents in his nose. The sheets were damp and musty, and when he looked around at the room, he experienced the unsettling feeling of not knowing where he was. This had happened to him many times before, and it always came as a rush of relief when his mind caught up with his body and he remembered. But this morning there was no rush of memory, and no relief.

He sat up slowly in the bed. He'd slept in his dressing gown, warm and snug, but his feet were exposed and cold as ice. The room was strange. He recognized that it was in his house—if it was nothing in the room, then it was the room's dimensions, the feel of the place beyond the door—but the furniture in there left him cold. A bed too small for him to sleep in, piles of bagged clothes in one corner, and a collection of dusty board games atop the wardrobe.

"What is this?" Ray said to the silence. It did not reply. His stomach rumbled and his bladder was full, and he quickly fled that room to piss.

Downstairs, his wet clothes from the night

before were piled in the corner of the kitchen. He made tea and stood at the back door, looking out at the grim wet day with the mug in his hand, nodding as the old woman from up the hill walked past and smiled at him. He'd been up the hill the previous night, looking for someone in the stormy darkness. He frowned, because he could not quite remember who.

After breakfast he dressed and, just as he was about to go downstairs again, he glanced once more into the strange room in which he'd woken up. It was empty to him. It echoed with something that should have been memory, but nothing quite struck home. He frowned, trying to clasp the memory. But all that came was a sense of bottomless sadness, its cause lost in darkness.

He ventured down to the village, steering himself without thought toward the bakery. On the way, turning a corner, he saw Wendy, the village untouchable. She pulled a tatty-wheeled shopping basket filled with her stuff for the day: cider, clothes, personal things.

They had never spoken to each other, but now she offered the saddest smile Ray had ever seen, as if she saw an unbearable truth still hidden to him. It brought a lump to his throat. She sighed and walked away.

Ray hurried on until he reached the bakery. Rachel smiled as he approached—she was laying out a display of cakes and freshly baked bread in the front window—but he could not find it in himself to smile back. He should have, he knew. Her young son had been poorly for a while, and though he thought he was better now, Ray should have still—

"Her young son," he said. Frowned. That was strange.

"Morning," Rachel said, coy and demure. "What can I get you this morning?"

"The usual," Ray said, because he could not remember what his usual was. He felt uncertain and unsettled. Something was missing, and it wasn't something about the village or its people. "Rachel . . . what's happened to me?"

"What?" she asked, looking him up and

down. The shy flirt had left her now. Perhaps being a single mother only ever allowed her the briefest opportunities, the shallowest flirts.

"Something happened, and I don't think I can remember what. There's a room in my house, and something's missing from it. It should matter to me. I slept in there last night, and . . ." He trailed off, shaking his head and wondering what her nervously flitting eyes meant.

"Are you . . . okay?" she asked.

"Yes. Yes, I'm fine." And he *was* fine. He felt a twinge of guilt when he eyed Rachel's breasts, but Elizabeth had left him. It had been long enough now to make it right for him to move on. There was that disturbing feeling, leftover from some strange dream, but he knew that would fade as the day wore on. So yes, he was fine.

Fine.

"That was Toby's room," Rachel said quietly.

"Toby," Ray said. Something pulsed within him—a surge of heat and pain, quickly fading.

He gasped softly, glanced around the bakery—empty but for him and Rachel—then back at the woman before him. "Who?"

"Ray?" she said.

"Toby who?" And he meant it. There'd been that reaction, like something passing through him. *Goose walking over your grave*, he heard his long-dead mother say, and he smiled at her precious memory.

"Ray?" Rachel said again.

Toby who? He turned and left the bakery without his bread and cakes. Rachel did not call him back, though he felt her watching him go. And the village felt hollow, like a thing of place and substance replaced with something light and false, and Ray felt a hollowness opening at the heart of him that was far larger than he could ever hope to understand.

He started walking, and the weight of that hollow place followed.

We see him walking away from the bakery, and perhaps from the hope he'd had for a new life. Inside, Rachel is watching him go, confused and a little scared. For months now she has been entertaining the idea of she and Ray becoming involved. She's dreamed about it, and sometimes fantasized, but now he is a stranger walking away, and she no longer knows his gait.

Ollie, precious to her, is her whole world. She'll not risk that world by becoming involved with someone. . . .

"Unhinged," she says. She starts whistling uncertainly as she lays out another tray of iced cake slices.

Outside, along the street, Ray walks. There's pain gone from his heart, but in its place is something worse. It's not always best to forget. Sometimes, to remember is all we have.

We should know. We've been doing this long enough, and remember it all: every loss, every breath of deceit, every illness and broken bone and impact of family fist on family flesh. It wears us down, and sometimes we drown beneath the weight of it all. But there's always that moment of *floating* when something works so well, and sadness is mended as easily as a broken toy.

We move quickly away from Ray who will grow to be our guilt—but we'll live with it—and away from Skentipple. Been there too long. Other places to go.

We drift inland far from the sea, until the solid weight of another place draws us down with the gravity of pain.

ABOUT THE AUTHOR

TIM LEBBON is a *New York Times*-bestselling writer from South Wales. He's had twenty novels published to date, including *The Island*, *The Map of Moments* (with Christopher Golden), *Bar None*, *Fallen*, *Hellboy: The Fire Wolves*, *Dusk*, and *Berserk*, as well as scores of novellas and short stories. He has won four British Fantasy Awards, a Bram Stoker Award, and a Scribe Award, and has been a finalist for the International Horror Guild and World Fantasy Awards. He has also been a judge for the World Fantasy Award. In 2004, *Fangoria* named him "one of the thirteen rising talents who promise to keep us terrified for the next twenty-five years." Only nineteen years left to go . . . better get busy.

Forthcoming books include *The Secret Journeys of Jack London* for HarperCollins (co-authored with Christopher Golden), *Echo City* for Bantam in the US and Orbit in the UK, *Coldbrook* for Corsair in the UK, *30 Days of*

Night: Fear of the Dark for Pocket Books, the massive short story collections *Last Exit for the Lost* from Cemetery Dance and *Ghosts and Bleeding Things* from PS Publishing, as well as several other projects not yet announced.

He has written several screenplays, and is currently developing two TV series with a British TV company.

Several of his novels and novellas are currently in development for screen in the USA and UK, and he is working on new novels and screenplays.

Find out more about Tim at his website: www.timlebbon.net